P9-CRO-403

Praise for *My Life in the Fish Tank*

"A carefully crafted blend of realism, age-appropriate sensibilities, and children's interests."
—Kirkus Reviews

"Instilled with humor, the plot offers a layered narrative with occasional verse, perfect for readers looking for something a little extra special. Realistic and sympathetic, this demonstrates a successful, meaningful, and responsible discussion around mental health for all ages. . . . Fans of *A Mango-Shaped Space* (2003) will devour and adore this novel."
—Booklist

"With sensitivity and skillful storytelling, Dee portrays a difficult subject in an engrossing, accessible way."
—Publishers Weekly

"I loved *My Life in the Fish Tank*. Once again, Barbara Dee writes about important topics with intelligence, nuance, and grace. She earned all the accolades for *Maybe He Just Likes You* and will earn them for *My Life in the Fish Tank* too."
—Kimberly Brubaker Bradley, author of *Fighting Words* and Newbery Honor Book *The War That Saved My Life*

Praise for *Maybe He Just Likes You*

"Mila is a finely drawn, sympathetic character
dealing with a problem all too common in middle school.
Readers will be cheering when she takes control!
An important topic addressed in an age-appropriate way."
**—Kimberly Brubaker Bradley, author of *Fighting Words* and
Newbery Honor Book *The War That Saved My Life***

"In *Maybe He Just Likes You*, Barbara Dee sensitively
breaks down the nuances of a situation all too common in our
culture—a girl not only being harassed, but not being
listened to as she tries to ask for help. This well-crafted
story validates Mila's anger, confusion, and fear,
but also illuminates a pathway towards speaking up
and speaking out. A vital read for both girls and boys."
**—Veera Hiranandani,
author of Newbery Honor Book *The Night Diary***

"Mila's journey will resonate with many readers, exploring a
formative and common experience of early adolescence that has
too often been ignored. Important and empowering."
**—Ashley Herring Blake, author of Stonewall Children's & Young
Adult Honor Book *Ivy Aberdeen's Letter to the World***

"*Maybe He Just Likes You* is an important, timeless story with funny, believable characters. Mila's situation is one that many readers will connect with. This book is sure to spark many productive conversations."

—Dusti Bowling,
author of *Insignificant Events in the Life of a Cactus*

"In this masterful, relatable, and wholly unique story, Dee shows how one girl named Mila finds empowerment, strength, and courage within. I loved this book."

—Elly Swartz, author of *Smart Cookie* and *Give and Take*

"*Maybe He Just Likes You* is the perfect way to jump-start dialogue between boy and girl readers about respect and boundaries. This book is so good. So needed! I loved it!"

—Paula Chase, author of *So Done* and *Dough Boys*

A *Washington Post* Best Children's Book
An ALA Notable Children's Book
A Project LIT Book Club selection
A Bank Street Best Children's Book

Also by **BARBARA DEE**

MY LIFE
in the
FISH TANK

BARBARA DEE

ALADDIN

New York   London   Toronto   Sydney   New Delhi

ALADDIN

An imprint of Simon & Schuster Children's Publishing Division
1230 Avenue of the Americas, New York, New York 10020
First Aladdin paperback edition September 2021
Text copyright © 2020 by Barbara Dee
Cover illustration copyright © 2020 by Jenna Stempel-Lobell
Also available in an Aladdin hardcover edition.
All rights reserved, including the right of reproduction in whole or in part in any form.
ALADDIN and related logo are registered trademarks of Simon & Schuster, Inc.
For information about special discounts for bulk purchases, please contact
Simon & Schuster Special Sales at 1-866-506-1949 or business@simonandschuster.com.
The Simon & Schuster Speakers Bureau can bring authors to your live event. For more information
or to book an event contact the Simon & Schuster Speakers Bureau at 1-866-248-3049 or visit our
website at www.simonspeakers.com.
Cover designed by Heather Palisi
Interior designed by Jess LaGreca
The text of this book was set in Odile.
Manufactured in the United States of America 0423 OFF
2 4 6 8 10 9 7 5 3
The Library of Congress has cataloged the hardcover edition as follows:
Names: Dee, Barbara, author.
Title: My life in the fish tank / Barbara Dee.
Description: First Aladdin hardcover edition. | New York, New York : Aladdin, 2020. |
Audience: Ages 9-13. | Summary: When twelve-year-old Zinnia Manning's older brother Gabriel is
diagnosed with bipolar disorder, it turns her family's world upside-down, especially since they are
keeping the information private.
Identifiers: LCCN 2020021831 (print) | LCCN 2020021832 (ebook) |
ISBN 9781534432338 (hardcover) | ISBN 9781534432352 (ebook)
Subjects: CYAC: Manic-depressive illness—Fiction. | Mentally ill—Fiction. | Brothers and sisters—
Fiction. | Family life—Fiction. | Friendship—Fiction. | Middle schools—Fiction. | Schools—Fiction.
Classification: LCC PZ7.D35867 My 2020 (print) | LCC PZ7.D35867 (ebook) | DDC [Fic]—dc23
LC record available at https://lccn.loc.gov/2020021831
LC ebook record available at https://lccn.loc.gov/2020021832
ISBN 9781534432345 (pbk)

For my family, with endless love

February 21

James Ramos got a haircut yesterday, but so what.

I mean, nothing against his hair: he had a perfectly regular-shaped head and un-clownish ears. And now you could see his eyes (brown), if that was super important to you.

But not to me. Unlike my two best friends, Kailani and Maisie, and probably a whole bunch of other girls in the seventh grade, I wasn't obsessed with James Ramos, or with his hair. So while we walked to school that morning, and Kailani went on and on about James Ramos And His Haircut, I tried to click on a different mental link.

Think about other stuff, I told myself.

The crayfish we're getting in science lab.

The fish tanks we're designing.

All the cool experiments we'll be doing—

Now Maisie tugged my jacket sleeve. "Don't you think, Zinny?" she was asking.

"About what, specifically?" I glanced at Kailani, hoping for a clue.

"That James likes Kailani! That he has a crush!"

"Oh, definitely," I said.

"Zinny." In the chilly air, Maisie's skin was pale, and her freckles stood out like punctuation marks. "No offense, but you're doing that thing again."

"What thing?"

"You know," Kailani said gently. "Tuning us out. Pretending we're not here."

"That's not true," I protested. "I mean, okay, sometimes my mind wanders a little—"

Maisie snorted. "Can I ask you something, Zinny? Why are you walking with us if you don't want to *be* with us?"

I couldn't answer that question.

Even though the words were all in my head:

But I do want to be with you.
To be honest,
with all the stuff going on in my family,
if I didn't have the two of you,
I couldn't go to school at all.

Six Months Earlier

"*Okay, gang, time to line up,*" *Dad says.*

The four of us groan, because groaning is part of it. Every late August, just before the start of school, Mom and Dad make us pose for the Annual Kid Photo. For this, Dad always takes out his old-fashioned digital camera ("This is not some cell phone picture," he says) and has us stand on the stairs, each of us on a separate step. We do it in size order, or maybe chronological: Gabriel on the bottom, then Scarlett, then me, with Aiden on the top, like the cherry on a sundae.

The Four Stages of Manning, Dad calls these photos. He always makes this joke, because our last name is Manning, and he likes to pun in a dad sort of way.

We roll our eyes.

But this time Scarlett protests. "You know, Dad, you shouldn't say the Four Stages of Manning like that means everybody. Because it doesn't."

"'Man' means man and woman," Gabriel tells her. "It's inclusive."

Gabriel is eighteen, just about to go off to college. His know-it-all streak drives Scarlett crazy.

"Bullcrap," Scarlett tells him. Although she doesn't say "crap."

"Scarlett," Mom says.

"Really, Mom, I just hate it when people say things like that! It's really offensive to other genders. Including women. And girls."

"I agree with Scarlett," I say loudly.

Scarlett flashes a smile and gives me a fist bump. She is sixteen, four years older than me, and her approval matters.

"Stop complaining, you two, and let me shoot this thing," Dad says, squinting. "Try to move forward a little, everybody. Aiden, bring your head closer to Zinny, and kind of lean into her."

"Then I'll lose my balance," I say.

"No you won't, Zinny. Lean into Scarlett."

"Yeah, Scar, but what's your point?" Gabriel asks. "You'd rather our last name was Manning-or-Wo-manning?"

"We don't need to make it binary," Scarlett says. "We could all just be Hu-manning."

My big brother laughs. "Well, hate to break it to you, but I'm not calling myself that!"

"How about if we get to choose our last name?" I say, laughing. "We can be Manning, Wo-manning, or Hu-manning!"

"How about if everyone stops talking nonsense and we get this picture over with?" Mom says in her teacher voice. Her high school students love her, I know, but she can be tough.

"Okay, fine," Scarlett says. "But please stop calling us the Four Stages of Manning, Daddy, because it isn't funny. And anyway, we're not stages of anything, because we're all separate human beings. And we're not turning into each other."

"That's called evolution," Aiden announces. "We learned about it in school."

"Already?" Scarlett asks, looking up over her shoulder at our little brother. She always seems surprised that Aiden isn't a baby anymore. "How did your teacher explain it—did she use the word 'man'?"

"I don't remember. I think there were pictures, anyway."

"Well, Aidy, if your teacher says 'man' to mean 'people in general,' you should tell her—"

Suddenly Gabriel slumps over and lets out a large grunt.

And because we've all been leaning into one another, we go sprawling.

"Gabriel, what was that?" Scarlett squeals.

He sticks out his bottom jaw. "I lowest step on evolution ladder! I Early Manning!"

Aiden starts giggling hysterically, the way he does only for Gabriel.

"Omigod, Gabriel!" Scarlett bops him on the head. "You're such a jerk! I can't believe we're even related!"

Mom frowns. "Guys, we can do this all day, if we have to," she warns. But her eyes are smiling. Even when Gabriel is clowning, wasting time, she's never mad at him, really.

A few seconds later, Dad snaps the photo. It's our best Annual Kid Photo ever, the four of us lined up again on the stairs, leaning into one another and laughing.

And, just a few months later, it's like the bottom step falls out.

No Month,
No Date, No Time

Sometimes I think we should have different systems for telling time. I mean like one system for when you go to school, hang out with your friends, play soccer on weekends, blahblahblah. We could call it something like Normal Standard Time.

But there would also be another system, another calendar completely, for when things get weird, or when bad things happen.

Because one thing you notice, when those bad things happen, is that calendars and clocks stop making any sense. Even if they still work perfectly okay, even if the batteries are good, and the cords are plugged in, and all you need to do is turn the page on the cute Rescue Dog of the Month calendar that's hanging on the fridge, they don't communicate anything useful. Or even anything your brain can understand.

At least that's how it seemed in our house.

It was like, after it happened, we were in a different time zone from everybody else.

A parallel universe.

And we needed some kind of new, not-yet-invented time measurement. Abnormal Standard Time.

Also a compass and a map.

Late November.
The Day It Happened.

It was strange how when it happened, we all sort of knew beforehand. Something about the way the phone rang that morning screamed *bad news*.

For one thing, it was the hour: five a.m. Who calls someone's house that early in the morning?

Unless it's an emergency.

So when the call came that Monday before Thanksgiving, we all jumped out of our beds. I mean that literally: we *jumped*. The whole family ran to the kitchen when Dad answered the phone, and we watched him nod and make small coughing sounds as he took out a pencil and pad from the phone shelf. "Yes," he kept saying. "When? I understand. Thank you."

He hung up and stared at us with hollow eyes. What had he been thanking the caller for? What did he understand?

"Tell us," Mom said breathlessly.

"It's Gabriel," Dad answered. "There's been an accident on campus."

Not: *He had an accident.*

There's been.

Mom's hand flew to her mouth.

"Is he okay?" I asked. "Where is he?"

"At the hospital, Zinny. Gabe wrecked his roommate's car, and he's a little banged up right now. He broke his collarbone, but they're saying he doesn't need surgery, and he'll just wear a sling for a while. He's lucky; sounds like from the condition of the car, it could have been much worse."

"Rudy wore a sling when he sprained his wrist," Aiden commented.

I gave my little brother a look that meant *Not now.*

"So they'll be releasing Gabriel from the hospital?" Mom asked. She was so pale it was hard to look at her.

I could see Dad working hard to breathe. "It's not

completely clear what the schedule is," he said, choosing his words one by one. "Apparently there were some concerns about Gabe's behavior in the emergency room."

"His *behavior*? What does that mean?" Scarlett demanded.

"I'm not sure. They just said he seemed a little off. We need more information." Dad took a second. "I have to drive up to campus now. Get Gabe's things from his dorm room and bring them to the hospital. I'm sure I'll know more when I'm there."

"I'm coming with you!" Mom cried out.

"Please, sweetheart," Dad begged. "Let me go by myself just now, sort things out a bit, and then you'll come."

Of everything he'd said, maybe this was the scariest. *Dad doesn't want Mom to come. Why not?*

But of course Mom insisted. And when she was set on something, there was no point arguing.

Ten minutes later they were in Dad's car, Mom shouting instructions out the window as they pulled out of the driveway. For dinner we could thaw the lasagna that was in the freezer. There was money in the cookie jar, in case we needed anything. Laundry in the dryer. Oh, and we should all have a good breakfast, watch the clock, and not be late for school.

"If she thinks I'm going to school today, she's crazy," Scarlett announced.

"Yeah, crazy," Aiden agreed. I didn't have the energy to argue with him, especially because I couldn't imagine going to school myself.

And before we knew it, the house started humming with people Mom must have called from the road. First it was her friends Carrie and Sondra, then assorted neighbors, some I'd met maybe once or twice in my whole life. Then Aiden's friend-turned-enemy Rudy, with his nosy mom, Mrs. Halloran. Then Kailani and Maisie, on their way to school.

They rang the doorbell, like always. As soon as they saw my face, they could tell it was something bad.

"What's going on?" Kailani asked in a scared voice.

"Gabriel," I answered, bursting into tears. And thinking how weird it was that I'd waited all this time to start crying.

My friends hugged me. Somehow they knew not to ask questions. I guess they weren't sure which questions to ask. Maybe they were afraid to hear my answers.

And Maisie always jumped at the chance to organize. "We'll tell the teachers you're going to be absent today," she said. "And we'll get all your assignments. Don't worry about school, Zinny."

"I'm not," I said, wiping my face with my hand.

Because why would I be thinking about my social studies homework, or today's math quiz, or any other school-related trivia, when in the all-important world of my family, my big brother, was—what was the expression Dad had used? "A little off."

Not just "a little banged up" from a car accident. Something else. Something worse.

Like he'd clicked a button and switched himself from the *on* setting—but just "a little." And really, the word "little" made no sense. Like in baseball: Either you were *on* base or *off*. Safe or out. Nothing in between.

Unless it was Dad's way of making it sound less serious. Although, from the way that phone call had sounded, he didn't know a whole lot anyway.

"Shouldn't we call them?" I asked Scarlett. By three o'clock our house had gone quiet; the grown-ups had all left to meet kids coming home from school. "Don't you think Mom and Dad know something by now?"

"When they have something to tell us, they'll *call*, Zinnia," Scarlett replied. "They *know* we're here waiting." She pressed her lips at me like I was being a selfish baby.

So I went to my desk and opened my laptop. Looking stuff up, especially science things, had a way of calming me sometimes. Because even if I didn't understand about black holes or why there's gravity, it was comforting to know that scientists did.

I typed "collarbone."

The collarbone, or clavicle, is the only bone that lies horizontally. It is the most commonly fractured bone in the human anatomy. Often the fractures are due to the force from a direct hit.

There were lots of skeleton drawings, but I couldn't look. It made me feel better, though, to read that collarbone fractures were common. The *most* common.

I waited all day for Mom and Dad to call with details.

The next time the kitchen phone rang, it was ten o'clock that night, Dad saying he and Mom were leaving the hospital and were on the way home.

Last Day of School, the June Before

"*Hey, Zinny? You up for a little celebration?*" *Gabriel is standing in my doorway, dressed in a faded Lakeland High School tee, tropical-flower shorts, and sunglasses. It's the last day of the school year, but he's dressed for mid-July, as if he's fast-forwarded a few weeks ahead of the rest of us.*

I'm still typing. "What for?" I ask.

"What for? You survived sixth grade! Don't you think that's a big deal?"

"I guess."

"Oh, come on, Monkeygirl! Sixth grade is a really long year! Let's go out for a little spin, just you and me. It's summer out, remember?"

I look up from my laptop. Kailani, Maisie, and I are having a group chat, but I can talk to them whenever. Hanging out with my big brother is special. And I can't think of the last time we went somewhere together, just the two of us.

"Okay," I say, gathering my long brown hair into a ponytail to get it off my sweaty neck. "What kind of celebration?"

Gabriel's hazel eyes are sparkling. "You decide. We're celebrating you."

"Really? Can we do Here's the Scoop?" It's the new ice cream shop, two towns over.

"Yeah, I was hoping you'd say that," he replies, grinning.

He drives us in Mom's car, blasting teen-boy music out the open windows. People on the sidewalk glare at us, but I don't care. I like that we're making noise. Once I even wave at a lady pushing a jogger stroller.

At Here's the Scoop, Gabriel orders a Monster Cone: three scoops of Rocky Road, plus whipped cream and hot fudge, plus sprinkles, in a giant waffle cone. I order a single scoop of cookie dough ice cream in a cup.

He can't believe it. "That's all? That's what we drove here for?"

Gabriel's voice is too loud. Louder than I've ever heard it in public. A mom at a table with twin toddlers looks up at us.

"It's my favorite flavor," I remind him.

"Then you should take a bath in it! Dump it over your head!"

I pretend to laugh. "What?"

He takes a giant mouthful of ice cream. "Come on, Zinny, at least order a Monster Cone. One little scoop doesn't celebrate anything!"

"He's right," says the scooper, a pretty purple-haired girl with dimples when she giggles. And when Gabriel grins back at her, I realize they're flirting with each other. Girls have always liked Gabriel; once when we were at the town pool, two older girls told me, "Your big brother is sooo cuuute." And I didn't know how to answer, so I swam away.

Suddenly I feel like I'm five years old.

"Okay, sure," I say, placing the cup of ice cream back on the counter. "Can you please make me a Monster Cone instead? With everything except whipped cream."

"Great choice," Gabriel says, slapping my back just a little bit too hard.

The scooper girl digs into the cookie dough ice cream again. But now I'm feeling on display, like I have something to prove. "Wait," I add. "Can we do cookie dough on the bottom, then raspberry chip, and chocolate brownie on top? And then hot fudge over everything? No sprinkles."

"Nice," says Scooper Girl, as if I've passed some kind of test.

Right at that moment, three kids Gabriel knows from school—a boy named Jack and two girls—walk in, and he shouts a hello, running over to hug them as if he hasn't talked to them in months. I've never seen him greet anyone like this, not even family. Scooper Girl is watching, and so is the mom with the twins. Then Gabriel announces he's treating all three school friends to Monster Cones, just like his. In fact, he insists on it. Also, he's getting another one for himself.

"Wait, what?" I speak quietly to my brother, because I don't want to embarrass him in front of the others. "Do you have enough money on you?"

"Oh, definitely, of course I do," he replies in the new too-loud voice he's been using since we got here. "Zinny, I have an idea. Why don't you wait for me outside?"

"Outside? But it's broiling. Why can't I stay in here?"

"Come on, I won't see these guys all summer, and they're my best friends. Well, some of my best friends! And we're all going to different colleges, so this is our last chance to hang, and you'll just feel awkward if you sit here listening. Don't worry, it'll be like five minutes, I swear."

I try to catch his eye, but now he's smiling at Scooper Girl. "It better not be longer than that," I mutter. "Just five minutes, okay?"

"Six at the most. I promise! Hey, you'd better eat your Monster Cone before it melts!"

So while Gabriel is inside in the air-conditioning with some of his best friends plus Scooper Girl, I'm outside, standing under a skinny tree that doesn't protect me from the sunshine. It's my first Monster Cone, and I want to make it last—but I can't see the cookie dough scoop anymore, probably because it's settled into the cone's bottom. Then the raspberry starts dripping down the sides, and as I try to keep up with the drips, the chocolate brownie scoop on top tilts at a weird angle.

Finally I give up trying to save it, and just eat the whole thing.

And wait for my brother, my hands and face sticky from sweat and ice cream. Why did Gabriel ask me to come, I wonder, if he doesn't want me with him? He's never treated me this way before, and I'm really annoyed.

Ten minutes pass. Fifteen.

At last Gabriel swings open the door, carrying what looks like a milkshake.

"Thanks for waiting," he says, grinning.

"Mmf," I say, letting him see my annoyance. "How can you possibly be drinking a shake after all that ice cream?"

"Thirsty," he answers. Practically shouts it at me.

We get into Mom's car and Gabriel turns on the AC full blast. Also the radio, even louder than before. BAMbambambamBAMbambam.

Then my brother flashes me a smile as bright as a Christmas tree. It makes me forgive him right away, although I don't tell him so.

"Hey, Monkeygirl," he shouts over the music, "you know what would make me incredibly happy right now? To go for a long, long drive. Me and you."

It's a relief that he wants to be with me now, just the two of us. I smile back. "Sure. Where should we go?"

"Nowhere. Everywhere. I just feel like moving. Don't you ever get that way, like you want to burst out of your skin?"

"I guess."

He opens the windows, even though the AC is on. We pull out of the parking spot with a vroom. "Yeah, and a lot of times when I'm driving, I get the best ideas. Like today, right this minute, you know what I'm thinking about? Tesla."

"You mean the electric car?"

"No, no, the inventor Nikola Tesla, who the car was named after. Don't you know about him, Zinny? The guy was a total genius—he figured out alternating current, which means he basically invented electric motors, and also fluorescent lights *and lasers and remote controls. Oh, and he invented the first hydroelectric power plant in Niagara Falls—isn't that amazing? Anyway, so what I've been wondering is, what did Tesla think before he figured out alternating current? Like, was he just sitting at his breakfast table eating a bagel and drinking a latte when all of a sudden he had this incredible brainstorm? Or was it he thought A, and then B, and if so C, which means D—you know, a logical order, one after the other, like dominoes? But if you saw the dominoes individually, you wouldn't think anything was special about them?"*

"I don't know," I say, wondering why my brother is speaking so fast, although probably it's from all the sugar. And I've never heard him talk about Tesla before. "I guess you could look it up. There must be a biography—"

"Oh, but biographies are useless, Zinny! They're all this kind of 'Then he went to school, and then he got married, and then he moved to this house' sort of crap, which doesn't tell you anything really important. I'm way more interested—no, I'm fascinated—with his mind, not his boring everyday life! Like what I wonder about, Zinny, and not just when I'm driving, is how did his mind work, how did he logically go from one idea to the next, you know what I'm saying? And what was he thinking about before he was thinking of reinventing the universe?

Because that's the stuff that if you could understand, who knows where it would lead you. Like it's an untapped source of energy, do you get what I'm saying?"

We turn off the street and screech onto the parkway. I stare out the window as trees zip by, one big blur of summer green.

Now I can feel my heart thudding and my palms sweating. This whole situation—my brother driving too fast, talking too loud about stuff I can't follow—is making me nervous. What's going on with him, anyway?

"Where are we going?" I ask.

"We're not going anywhere," Gabriel answers, laughing, as his foot hits the gas. "That's the whole point of what I'm trying to explain to you: just turning the wheels on a beautiful summer day! Oh, and the same thing for Thomas Edison—"

"What same thing?"

"You know, how did his mind work before he invented the light bulb? And when he did invent the light bulb, did a light bulb go off in his head? Haha, it couldn't have, right? Because he hadn't invented it yet! So maybe it was a sundial or a torch or what do you call that thing, oh right, a candelabra—"

"I want to go home," I blurt.

"Now?" He turns to look at me, a second too long. His eyes are wide, shocked.

"Watch the road!" I yell.

"I am, Zinny! I'm totally watching the road! You don't have to tell me to do that, okay? We just passed the sign that said Lakeland—"

"Gabriel, you're going too fast! And this isn't fun. Let's just go home now. Please!"

He doesn't answer. Or slow down.

My fingernails dig into the seat. "GABRIEL!"

The car swerves to take an exit.

"Fine, Zinny!" my brother snaps. "If that's what you want to do, that's what we'll do. Although I thought you weren't a boring baby who only wanted to sit in her room and chat with her friends all day long, even though it's summer. But I guess I was wrong about you!"

This stings. But by now I'm just closing my eyes, trying to tune him out, not hear the blaring music or feel the wind whipping my hair out of the ponytail.

For the rest of the ride, Gabriel doesn't say a word. The silence between us feels like an electrified fence.

When we get home a few minutes later, he doesn't seem angry with me anymore, just tired. He turns off the car ignition and gives a small sheepish grin.

"Sorry I said all that before," he says. "You're not a baby."

I shrug. "It's okay."

"Well, but I feel bad that I called you that. You're not mad at me, Zinny?"

"I was, but not anymore. Are you mad at me?"

"Nah." He does the full Gabriel smile. "Hey, so can I ask you a big favor? About these." He dangles the car keys.

"Wait." I'm staring at him, trying (again) to understand what he's telling me. "You took Mom's car keys? Without permission?"

"Kind of. She was out running. And her keys just were sitting there on the kitchen counter, and I had to get out of the house—"

"Oh, Gabriel." He's gotten in trouble for this before. Mom is fine with him driving her car, but she has a thing about communication, especially from him. "If you want the car keys, just ask," she says all the time.

And I can't help thinking: It would have been bad enough if we'd gone to Here's the Scoop and come straight back home. But the way he kept going on that road, driving until I made him stop, only made it more likely Mom would find out. And be furious.

Why would he risk that? None of it made any sense—the driving, the talking. Even all the ice cream.

"So are you gonna tell Mom on me?" Gabriel is asking, not looking at me.

"No," I say. He called me a baby; even though he took it back, I definitely don't want to be called a tattletale, too. "I'm not going to tell. But Gabriel—"

"Thanks, Monkeygirl," he says, and then he slams the car door behind him.

Un-time

After that phone call on Monday, time got weird for us. It was almost like everything froze. Like the rest of the world was still liquid, flowing, but inside our house everything had turned to ice. Nothing changed or moved. We were in another dimension from everybody else, where minutes and hours went by, but they didn't count somehow. Anyway, none of us added any notes to the Rescue Dog of the Month kitchen calendar. And when November ended (a brownish mutt named Bonkers), nobody turned the page to December (a one-eared shepherd mix named Pablo).

Mom and Dad kept driving back and forth, to and from

the hospital, even on Thanksgiving. At some point during those drives, Mom quit her teaching job. She just told us she was "taking some time away," but not how long that would be. And when she was home, early in the morning and late at night, she was constantly researching on her computer, or arguing with insurance companies on her phone. So I started to think that this was her new job: arranging doctor stuff for Gabriel.

Who Scarlett, Aiden, and I hadn't seen since the accident.

And who we hadn't heard anything about.

Still.

"Not yet," Mom and Dad kept telling us whenever we asked about visiting. "Soon."

But when would that be, exactly? "Soon" wasn't real time. It was Abnormal Standard Time, like "some time away." And I began to wonder if it would ever happen.

Scarlett, Aiden, and I didn't go to school the day after Gabriel's accident, mostly because (despite all the neighbors bringing over casseroles and pies and pointlessly "checking in") nobody was forcing us—and then it was the four-and-a-half-day Thanksgiving weekend. So basically for that entire week the three of us just slept late,

ate Cheerios at noon, played video games, got dressed, ate chocolate chip cookies, played more video games, took naps.

Maisie and Kailani texted a few times to ask if I wanted company. But the truth was I didn't; I just wanted to be with Scarlett and Aiden. The odd thing was how we did everything together, like we were afraid to let one another out of our sight. Like we were still standing on the stairs, leaning into one another, afraid we'd go sprawling if any of us made a sudden move.

Except once, Scarlett sneaked away, locked herself in the bathroom, and cut her hair with a pair of nail scissors. The haircut was really short and raggedy-looking, like how a little girl would wreck her doll. Maybe she thought it looked cool or goth, or it was supposed to be a statement about her feelings, or something, but I thought she just looked awful.

I mean, I was proud of my thick brown hair. It had taken me two years—since fifth grade—to grow it long enough to make a good ponytail, or sometimes to wear it in braids.

"Why did you do that to your hair?" I asked.

"Because it's *my hair*," Scarlett growled at me. "I don't need you to understand."

Good, because I don't, I answered her in my head.

Sunday after Thanksgiving, Eight Thirty P.M.

Mom and Dad called Scarlett, Aiden, and me into the living room. Mom sat on the sofa, petting the cushion next to her for Aiden to sit there. Dad sat where he usually did, in the old gray easy chair. Scarlett perched on the ottoman, and I picked the sofa arm, to Mom's right.

"Okay," Dad said. He cleared his throat. "We wanted to update you guys about Gabriel."

"Yeah, about time," Scarlett muttered.

Dad flinched. "Scarlett, we haven't been hiding things to be mean or unfair. We've just had a lot to sort out, a bunch of meetings with Gabe's doctors. Also with a few of his professors and several of his classmates. And we wanted to get a better handle on the sequence of events."

Sequence of events.

"What's going on with Gabriel?" I asked in a small voice.

"Right now he's still recovering from the car accident," Mom said. "The doctors think he'll be discharged from the hospital very soon. So that's good news."

There was a pause.

Why is there a pause?

My heart was in my throat. "And then he'll go back to college?" I asked.

Mom and Dad exchanged a look I hadn't seen before.

"No, sweetheart," Mom said slowly. "We didn't really understand all this before now, but Gabriel has something else, a type of disorder that caused the accident. And a few other things—"

"*Other things?* Like what?" Scarlett demanded.

"Some behavior people noticed on campus," Dad said. "We don't need to go into specifics right now. But apparently, with the end of the semester, Gabe's been under a lot of stress. And not sleeping—"

"Dad, that's normal college stuff," Scarlett protested. She was a high school junior, so she knew about things like this.

Mom took a deep breath. "No, honey. It's more serious than that. His roommate told us that before the accident Gabriel was sleeping all the time, not talking to anyone, skipping classes. Then lately he'd stopped sleeping altogether, and was just typing around the clock. And he wouldn't stop talking and laughing—so loudly the kids next door complained."

"Okay, but that doesn't mean anything," Scarlett said. "Gabriel's always been loud and silly! And all the typing—he was probably just meeting deadlines at the end of the semester! You know how he puts everything off until the last minute."

"Also," Dad said, "we hear your brother's been drinking and driving, way too fast. Which is how he smashed up his roommate's car."

"That's impossible," I blurted. "I mean, okay, sometimes he drives too fast, but he *knows* about drinking—"

Mom closed her eyes for a second. I could see she didn't want to talk about the roommate's car. "We heard Gabriel was acting pretty wild when they brought him to the emergency room, yelling at everyone, making a scene. The doctors think he may have something called bipolar disorder. But it's completely treatable—"

"What?" Aiden said. It was as if he'd been playing Nintendo inside his head the whole time, and only now realized we were having a conversation. This conversation. "What's wrong with Gabriel?"

"Gabriel has a mental illness, baby," Mom said.

"He does not."

"Yes, Aiden, he does. It's like his moods are stronger than other people's, and he can't control them. Sometimes he's very happy or angry for no reason, and sometimes he's sad and sleepy for no reason. It's not his fault, sweetheart." She caught her breath. "But if he goes to a special type of hospital for a while, where he can get medicine and therapy—"

"You're sending him somewhere *else*?" Suddenly Scarlett sprang up from the ottoman. "This is so wrong, Mom! Gabriel's fine—he's just being stupid and selfish, like he always is, making everyone pay attention! I don't care about his typing, or his loudness, or his sleep habits, and I don't want to hear this anymore!"

She ran out of the living room. I could hear the door to our bedroom slam shut.

"Oh boy," Dad said.

"She'll be okay," Mom said. "I'll talk to her." Then she pretended to smile at Aiden and me. "Okay, guys, we'll continue this conversation another time. Right now the two of you should get ready for school in the morning."

"We're going back tomorrow?" Aiden asked. "What about Scarlett?"

"She's going back too."

What about you, Mom? I wanted to ask. *Aren't you going back to school, also?*

But I already knew the answer. And right then Mom and Dad both looked exhausted, like talking about Gabriel had sucked up all their energy.

I turned to Aiden, whose eyes were huge and round. "Well, *I* want to go back to school," I announced. "I can't wait, actually."

"Me too," Aiden said, although I could tell he was just playing Follow the Leader.

"Oh, one other thing," Mom said as she stood. "Dad and I discussed this, and we'd like us all to try to keep this private. For Gabriel's sake."

"You mean secret?" I asked.

"Not secret, private," Dad said. He flashed Mom a look.

"Okay," I said.

But if there was a difference between those two words—"secret" and "private"—I didn't know what it was.

First Week of December

It wasn't a lie: I really *was* relieved to go back to school. All the things about it that used to drive me crazy— the dumb quizzes, the gossip, the way people cared what other people were wearing and who they were sitting with at lunch—were perfect distractions now. Things to fill my head. And my head had more space to fill than I'd ever realized before.

At first they made me see the school psychologist, Dr. Godrich, a nice woman with a murmury voice and black eyeliner. Dr. Godrich kept asking how I was "doing," how my parents were "coping," if there was anything I wanted to "share." "About what?" I asked, as if I had no idea what she meant. "About anything," she replied, making her face go blank. It was kind of like the two of us were playing Chicken, and the first person to say Gabriel's name would lose. So we just talked about homework, and what my plans were for winter break, and eventually I stopped getting called to Dr. Godrich's office.

Maisie and Kailani also talked about Anything But Gabriel. Maybe they thought if they kept chattering about James Ramos, Who Might Have a Crush on Kailani, they could reverse time for me, in a way. But of course that was impossible. And I knew it, even if they didn't.

Finally, at the end of that week, they brought up Gabriel. Not directly. Sort of sideways.

"Are you okay, Zin?" Kailani asked. "I mean, *really* okay?"

The three of us were in the cafeteria, a few feet away from everyone else. I could see worry in Kailani's big, dark eyes.

"Yeah," I said. "Don't I seem okay?"

"Actually, you do." She looked down at her burrito. "Maybe a little *too* okay."

I chomped on my apple. "What does that mean?"

Kailani's skin was brown; I couldn't always tell when she was blushing. But this time I could. I saw her eyes lock with Maisie's, then look down at her burrito. Again.

"Zin," Maisie said, slowly and carefully, as if the two of them had rehearsed this. "We just want you to know that if you ever *do* want to talk about your brother . . . I mean, you don't *have* to, or anything. But if you ever *did*. You know we're both totally here for you, right?"

"Sure," I said. Were they asking me to cry? Here, in the middle of the lunchroom, where everyone could see? I could feel my throat starting to burn. "I definitely know that. And I will. Talk to you guys, I mean."

"Promise?" Kailani asked in a soft voice. Finally she'd lifted her eyes to look right at me.

"Yeah," I said. "Promise."

They exchanged another look. And that was when I understood that I'd disappointed them. Like they'd been expecting me to tell them everything about Gabriel—maybe not what had happened with the car, specifically, or even how he'd gone "a little off," but how I felt about it. How we all felt about it. But that was not something I could do, especially not right here, in front of the whole seventh grade.

Mostly because of what Mom had said—how we needed to keep Gabriel "private." But also because I was thinking:

You could say *My brother is crazy,* and nobody would blink, probably. But if you said *Okay, here's the truth: my brother is mentally ill, so my parents sent him to a sort-of-hospital,* who knew what would happen? I'd never heard anyone say those words, at school or anywhere else.

And if I said all that, maybe people would start to wonder about *me.* One thing I was sure of: if you said that sentence—*my brother is mentally ill, so my parents sent him to a sort-of-hospital*—it wouldn't end the conversation. There'd be a million questions and follow-ups: *How long will he be there? Will he ever be okay? What if he goes crazy again?* But it wasn't like I had any answers. Or would be allowed to say them, even if I knew.

Besides, the whole point of school was to let me *not* think about it. To let me think about other things instead— locker combinations, French pronouns, the way our math teacher, Mr. Halverson, always had a snot drop at the end of his nose. Maybe it would fall off, and maybe it wouldn't; sometimes I'd spend the period watching it, waiting for it to plop on someone's desk. Or for Mr. Halverson to notice it was happening and get himself a tissue.

Anyway, right after that, Maisie switched topics to Aspen Garber, who might have been staring at James

Ramos during math, whatever *that* was supposed to mean. And even though usually the topic of James Ramos made me switch mental channels, I leaped into the conversation.

"Oh yeah, Aspen *wishes* James Ramos liked her," I declared. "But ha. *We* know he likes Kailani."

Besides being a distraction from home, the other good thing about school was science class. Our teacher, Ms. Molina, had a lab next door to her classroom where she kept all sorts of incredible things and creatures in small glass tanks—a hissing cockroach, a praying mantis, a box of shark teeth. Along the window ledge were alien-looking plants with names she liked saying: *Kalanchoe tomentosa. Echeveria elegans. Schlumbergera bridgesii.*

Science was right after lunch. So sometimes if I got to class early, Ms. Molina would let me poke around her lab for a few minutes. She never tried to force me to chat about schoolwork, or even checked up on "how things are going" in that teachery sort of way. She just let me look at stuff, every once in a while making random comments like, "The cockroach is off carrots lately; think I'll try some bananas," and "Wouldn't it be cool to get an axolotl?"

Being in Ms. Molina's lab reminded me of something,

somewhere happy, but at first I couldn't figure out what.

Then I remembered.

A vacation trip to Chicago, four years ago. All six of us at the Art Institute, where they have something called the Thorne Miniature Rooms—little shoebox-size rooms from different periods in history, decorated with fancy carved furniture and beautiful tapestries and so much detail you feel like moving right in. I mean, you could if you shrank yourself thumb-size.

At first Gabriel grumbles about us going there. "It's like some boring tiny dollhouse," he says. "For girls."

"Omigod, you did not just say that," Scarlett growls at him.

But after a few minutes, Gabriel admits the exhibit is incredible. He even takes a selfie of the two of us—him and me—in front of the mini room that is supposed to be a French Revolution bathroom.

"It's like Bathroom World!" Gabriel exclaims. "Although what would be really awesome would be a mini Dunkin' Donuts bathroom! With a teeny-tiny liquid soap dispenser. And a little bitty hand dryer. And microscopic graffiti—"

"Shh," Mom scolds him in her teacher voice. "Museum voices, please."

But the two of us—Gabriel and I—keep laughing way too

loudly, adding other bathrooms it would be hilarious to see on display: the one at Thom's Pizza, the one at the gas station, even the kids' bathroom in our house. I think of myself as a person who notices things, but I can't keep up with Gabriel, who seems to have a photographic memory when it comes to bathroom details: spooky motion-detector paper-towel dispensers, weird flushing handles, faucets that refuse to turn off, whatever you do.

Afterward, we go to the museum gift shop, and Gabriel surprises me with a present—a tiny chair, the size of a Monopoly token, that looks like the ones in the French Revolution bathroom.

"Thanks, but what am I supposed to do with this?" I ask him.

"Nothing, Monkeygirl," he says, giving me a goofy grin. "It's a good-luck charm."

"Okay, but I don't believe in luck."

"Yeah? Well, maybe you should."

And after that lunch with Maisie and Kailani, when our social studies teacher was going on and on about research tools and bibliographies, and also during French class and math, I had this weird feeling like I'd shrunk myself thumb-size. And I wasn't in my actual real life—which had a Gabriel-size hole in the middle of it, a hole so big it would suck you in if you even leaned in its direction—but in a miniature room somewhere, a tiny diorama, where tiny me was sitting at a tiny desk, taking notes, caring about all the things you were supposed to care about in that pretty, miniature world. And I couldn't just leave, because people had come from all over, and had paid admission, and were lining up to watch me pretend.

Third Week of December, Right before Winter Break

S carlett never officially kicked me out of our bedroom. But a month after Gabriel's accident, it was clear that every day after school, and every evening, my sister expected to have our room all to herself. Which felt like she was pushing me away.

I mean, it wasn't like I was assuming that we'd talk about Gabriel, because I could tell she still didn't believe he was actually sick. But the way Scarlett made it clear that she wished I was somewhere else kind of hurt my feelings. Also bothered me, because it was my room too.

And it wasn't just the not-talking-about-Gabriel that

was making things weird between us. Scarlett never joked around with me anymore, or asked about my friends, or tried to tease me about which boy I liked (obviously not James Ramos). Her teasing used to drive me crazy, but now that she shot eye-daggers if I tried to chat about anything, I definitely missed the old annoying Scarlett.

But I couldn't force her to be that old way with me— and the new way was giving me a stomachache. Finally I relocated my laptop to the dining room to hang out with Aiden, who'd just started having serious homework. It used to be Mom who kept Aiden company while he did his math worksheets and practiced penmanship. But since Gabriel's accident, she'd either been napping on the sofa in the afternoons, or in her bedroom yelling at insurance companies on her cell.

Aiden never asked anyone else for help, or complained that Mom was ignoring him—but I couldn't help thinking he seemed a little lost, with all his workbooks and notebooks and pencils dumped all over the table. So after a few minutes of watching him stare at a book while he sipped a juice box, I asked what he was reading.

"It's research," he said, his eyes still on his book. "For a big project after winter break. It's not due for a long, long time, but Ms. Felsenstein says we should start thinking."

"Really?" I tried to remember if we'd "researched" things back when I was in third grade. But that whole year was kind of a blur, just a bunch of spelling tests and birthday parties. "What's the project?"

"Well, it's supposed to be a how-to," Aiden said.

"How to do what?"

He finally looked up at me. "It's up to us. But we need to describe it step-by-step."

"Awesome," I said. "I could help you think up a topic. You could do How to Bake Bread. Or How to Tie a Tie."

He sipped his apple juice. "Thanks, Zinny, but I already picked something."

"Yeah? What?"

"How to Survive Quicksand."

For some reason, I flinched at that.

"Why?" I challenged him. "I mean, why *that*, of all topics?"

"Because it's interesting." He held up a chewed-looking paperback with the cover half ripped off. "I'm reading about it, Zinny. There's a special method."

"Seriously?"

"Yeah. First you're supposed to drop everything you're holding, like a backpack. Then you take off your shoes."

"Your *shoes*? Aiden, if you're in quicksand, the last thing you care about is saving your shoes."

"No, it's not about *saving* them. Shoes create suction, especially boots. So if you take them off in time, it helps you to float on top. Then you lie back, like this." He made his hand horizontal. "The more you spread out, the harder it is to sink. And if you have a walking stick, you keep it underneath you. Like this." He held a pencil under his hand.

"Okay, but who actually uses a walking stick?"

"Explorers. They're *supposed* to."

I studied my little brother's face. His brown eyes were huge and his mouth looked pinched, like he was sucking an invisible straw.

"Aiden, you're not actually worried about this, are you?" I asked. "Because it's not like quicksand ever happens around here."

"But it could," he insisted. "It can happen *anywhere*. See?" He opened his book and handed it to me.

I read:

Quicksand is a real phenomenon. Just about any sand or silt can temporarily become quicksand if it is sufficiently saturated with water or subjected to vibrations, such as those that occur during an earthquake.

"Yeah, but." I pushed the book back at him. "It's incredibly rare, you know? Like a one-in-a-billion chance of happening, and definitely not in Oregon. Shouldn't you pick a topic that isn't so . . . out there?"

Aiden's lower lip pouted. Suddenly I had a picture of how he looked to other people, the kind of kid who could burst into tears at any minute. And that was when it hit me that he'd been spending every afternoon alone, with his homework and his juice boxes. Never having after-school play dates, the way you usually did in third grade.

"Trust me, Aiden," I said. "If there was quicksand around here, I'd definitely have stepped in some by now. Although we do have potholes." I smiled encouragingly. "Maybe you can do that: How to Survive Falling into a Pothole."

"That's just boring, Zinny."

"No, it's not! It's useful! Or what about How to Survive If You Step in Dog Poop. Or a Wad of Bubble Gum."

He shook his head.

"Or How to Survive When a Squirrel Falls Down Your Chimney and Knocks Over the Christmas Tree. Remember when that happened?"

"Nobody else cares about that," Aiden said. "Just our family. Anyhow, I'll have to say the how-to in front of the whole class, so it needs to be cool."

"Come on, Aiden. That squirrel was *extremely* cool."

I considered reminding Aiden how Gabriel had dressed up as Santa and lured the squirrel into a sack of gingerbread. But Aiden crossed his arms and shook his head. He didn't want to hear it.

"Okay," I said. "So how about this: How to Survive an Attack of *Flying Squirrels*."

"Flying squirrels attack?"

"Not really," I admitted. "That's why it's a funny topic."

"Okay," Aiden said doubtfully. I could tell he was thinking. Suddenly his eyes lit up. "Or How to Survive a Scorpion That Sneaks into Your Juice Box When You Aren't Looking."

I grinned. "Exactly. Perfect! Or how about How to Survive If You're in a Wind Tunnel Full of Frogs."

"Yeah," Aiden said. "Frogs *and toads*." He was giggling now.

"Or what about How to Survive When You're Stuck in an Elevator with a Person Who Uses Too Much Perfume."

"Yeah, I hate that. Or How to Survive If Zombies Attack You on a Ferris Wheel."

"You mean the zombies climb up the Ferris wheel while it's moving?"

"No, Zinny, they're in the next car. And you didn't know it."

"Ah," I said. "And you mean all of a sudden they lean over . . ."

"Yeah. And attack! While the whole thing is spinning around really fast." Aiden rotated his arm, knocking some papers off the table.

"Okay, now *that's* a great topic," I said, laughing. "You could research Ferris wheel speeds."

"Also zombies!"

"What's all the laughing in here?" Mom was standing by the table, blinking as if her eyes weren't used to daylight. Maybe after yelling at the insurance companies, she'd been napping; she'd gotten home from the hospital very late last night.

"Sorry, Mom," I said quickly. "We'll try to keep it down."

"No, honey, I'm not telling you to be quiet. But what's so funny?"

Aiden and I looked at each other.

"Zinny was just helping me with homework," he said, all the smiling gone from his eyes. "But now I need to get back to work."

He returned the quicksand book to his lap, took a long sip of juice, and started reading.

Christmas, Two Years Ago

Christmas morning starts with a crash.

As soon as we hear it, Scarlett and I leap out of our beds and run into the living room. Gabriel is standing there, staring at our Christmas tree, which is now smashed against the rug. Most of the ornaments are still stuck to the branches, but some of them (the glass icicles, the gold tin balls) have been shaken loose, shattered all over the room.

"What happened?" Scarlett asks.

"No idea," Gabriel answers. "I was just in the kitchen having breakfast, and all of a sudden, thwump."

"Trees don't just fall over all by themselves, Gabriel!"

"Yeah, Scarlett, obviously. Are you saying I went, 'Ooh, here's a fun idea, while everyone else is asleep, why don't I go over and knock it down'?"

"Well, no," she admits. "But since you were the only one up—"

Suddenly something whooshes by my feet. A small brown furry thing. I scream.

"Omigod, what was that?" Scarlett yells. She flings herself onto the sofa.

Now Aiden is in the living room. "How come there's a squirrel in our house?" he asks, as if he thinks there could be a logical answer.

"That was a squirrel?" I squeal. "Are you sure, Aiden? How do you know?"

"Because it had a bushy tail. And a squirrely head—"

"Don't say 'squirrely head.'" I shudder. I am all in favor of squirrels, and rodents in general, but only in their natural habitats.

"I bet it came in through the chimney," Gabriel says. A smile is creeping across his face. "Hoping we'd mistake it for a reindeer. It probably has glued-on antlers and a fake red nose. But squirrel-size."

"Stop!" Scarlett yells. "This is not funny!" But she's smiling too.

"Well, we have to catch it, don't we?" I say. "I mean, we can't just let it run loose all over the house!"

"Come on, Zinny," Gabriel says. "It's just spreading Christmas cheer." He does his goofy Gabriel smile at me.

Which of course means I have to smile back at him.

Then Mom and Dad are standing beside us in clashing plaid bathrobes.

"What the hell—" Dad begins.

"It's the Squirrel of Christmas Present," Gabriel says. "Our theory is he accidentally knocked over the tree."

"Use 'they' if you're not sure of gender," Scarlett reminds him.

Mom groans. "Guys, I told you I was against hanging gingerbread stars. I bet the squirrel was attracted to the scent."

"You mean they smelled cookies from outside?" Scarlett asks. "And then snuck in to steal one from the tree? Mom, I bet squirrels don't even like gingerbread—"

"Forget about the gingerbread," Dad says. "Let's just send it back into the great outdoors. Pronto. Where's a broom?"

"Don't say 'it,' and don't sweep him!" Aiden shouts. "Squirrels aren't garbage!" The way his chin is quivering, I can tell he's trying not to cry.

"Can't we just call a wildlife person?" Mom begs.

"It's Christmas morning," Dad reminds her. "If anyone's working, they'll just charge extra. Gabriel, what are you doing?"

Gabriel has slipped out of the living room, and now he returns in a fuzzy, baggy Santa suit, carrying a red felt sack. This is Dad's costume he used to put on for us when we were little. Now it smells dusty, like the garage, where Dad tossed it a few years ago. Maybe he'd decided he was too old for holiday dress-up, or too tired, or something.

"Ho-ho-ho," Gabriel booms. He tosses some smashed gingerbread stars into the sack, which he sets by the sliding doors. "Come and get it, Rudolph."

Sometimes Gabriel doesn't explain things very well. Or at all. And once again I have the feeling I need to pin him down, just to be sure I'm following.

"You're going to lure the squirrel into the sack?" I ask. "And then free him—I mean them—outdoors, right?"

"Yep," he says. "It's the festive thing to do."

"Well, it won't come if we all stand around watching," Mom says. "I think it needs privacy."

"Just like Santa does," Aiden says. He's six, at the age when either he knows about Santa or he doesn't. And because he's the baby of the family, none of us want to spoil it for him.

"Want some help?" Dad asks Gabriel. He doesn't seem too enthusiastic.

"Nah," Gabriel tells him. "This is a job for Santa."

The rest of us clear out of the living room. About fifteen minutes later we hear scuffling, then another crash, then Gabriel shouting, "Hey, rodent, over here," then more scuffling. Then the sound of doors sliding open and shut.

"Ho-ho-ho, everybody!" Gabriel shouts. "Rudolph's gone down in history!"

We rush back into the living room. Gabriel's face is flushed, and he's beaming.

"You let him back outside?" Aiden asks. "Rudolph's okay?"

"Are you kidding, buddy?" Gabriel is laughing, mussing Aiden's hair. "Rudolph's better than okay. Right now he's bragging to all his squirrel friends how he knocked down a tree, then ate a sackful of gingerbread. It's the best day of his whole squirrel life!"

Late December

A few days before Christmas, Gabriel left the hospital and came home. Except it wasn't really Gabriel. It was some paper-cutout version of him, thinner and flatter than my real brother.

As soon as he stepped into the front hallway with Mom and Dad, I hugged him through his down jacket—a small sideways hug, careful to avoid the sling strapped across his body.

"Hey, you," he said quietly.

"Hey, you back," I said, smiling. "We're so glad you're home again! Finally!"

"And you didn't even miss Christmas!" Aiden shouted.

Gabriel flinched, like he wasn't used to loud voices. "You're right, buddy, I didn't. Although I don't have presents for anyone."

"Then you're not getting any from us," Scarlett teased.

Everybody laughed except Gabriel. I knew we were just nervous, but I couldn't help thinking this welcome-home had gone wrong somehow.

"Well, if it's okay, I think I'll go lie down now," Gabriel said. "That car trip wore me out."

"Oh sure," Dad said quickly. "I could use a nap myself!"

Mom didn't take her eyes off Gabriel. "Sweetheart, don't you want a little snack first? I baked a whole tray of gingerbread—"

"No, thank you," Gabriel said. His voice sounded hollowed out. Too polite.

Scarlett and I traded a look.

After that Gabriel stayed inside his room, sleeping. He didn't eat very much either. Not even Mom's gingerbread.

Two days after Christmas, Mom and Dad drove him to a place called Redwoods Village. It wasn't actually a hospital, Dad explained, it was a "residential treatment center," but I wondered if those were just words you said, like "a little off."

Right before they left, I asked Mom why Gabriel couldn't just live with us.

Mom was in her bedroom, packing a small overnight bag and sniffling into a tissue. She added a pretend cough, like she was trying to convince me she had a cold, but of course I knew she'd been crying. "Your brother needs a lot of support right now, sweetheart. The doctors have to get him stable on his meds, and that's a whole complicated process. And he needs intensive therapy."

"Can't he get therapy here?"

"Not as much as he can get at Redwoods Village."

She tried to smile, but it didn't work. As her eyes filled with tears that she dabbed away with the crumpled tissue, I couldn't watch. "Also, honey, at this point Gabriel needs round-the-clock supervision. For his own safety."

"Okay," I said, and escaped the bedroom.

The name Redwoods Village sounded cheery, even Christmasy. But after that conversation I was pretty sure what it was. A sort-of-mental-hospital where your brother got sent, and they wouldn't let him leave.

After Winter Break

At lunch Kailani and Maisie were discussing Guess Who again, whether some comment he made in homeroom meant he was dropping out of orchestra. What James Ramos did with his viola was about as interesting to me as belly-button lint. And I was positive that if I heard one more word on that topic, my brain would turn into soup and leak out both of my ears.

So while they talked, I wrote a mental list to share with Aiden:

How to Survive If You Take a Bite of Pizza and Realize the Cheese Is Molten Lava

How to Survive If You Sit on a Rock but It's
   Actually a Snapping Turtle
How to Survive If Overnight All the Floors in Your
   House Turn to Jell-O
How to Survive If It's Raining Saliva
How to Survive If You're Lost in the Arctic and All
   You Have for Ice Fishing Is a Wire Coat Hanger
How to Survive If Your Friends Won't Shut Up
   About James Ramos

"Okay," I blurted. "I need to go see Ms. Molina!"

Maisie's blue eyes got big. "Again? Zinny, you go there almost every lunch."

"I just want to ask her something."

"Can't it wait?" Kailani asked. "Lunch isn't over for twelve more minutes. And then we won't see you until dismissal."

Maisie and Kailani were both Team West. I was Team East. We were together for homeroom and lunch, but that was it.

"I know, but." I shrugged. "I really like hanging out with Ms. Molina."

Kailani and Maisie traded a look. Saying you liked hanging out with a teacher—in fact, that you *preferred* it to hanging out with your best friends—was just plain weird, and we all knew it.

"Zinny, can I please just say something?" Maisie said. "I mean, we haven't brought it up, because we don't want to pressure you. But lately you've been acting kind of . . . strange."

"What do you mean?" I sipped some water.

"You never want to do anything with us after school anymore. You barely talk to us when we're together. And basically you act like you're on another planet."

I felt my stomach flip. Because they were sort of making me sound like Gabriel. And who knew, maybe Gabriel's college friends had said almost the exact same words to him before his accident.

Am I like Gabriel?

Why wouldn't I be? And Scarlett and Aiden, too, for that matter.

"We know you're worried about your brother," Maisie added quickly. "I mean, how can you not be? But my mom says he's doing better from that car accident, right?"

Her *mom*? What did she know about anything? I couldn't imagine Mom telling Maisie's mom; they weren't close. Unless Mom had talked about Gabriel to one of her friends, and then that friend had blabbed to someone else . . .

But I thought we were supposed to keep Gabriel's illness "private." All of us, including Mom.

"Yeah, he's recovering," I said, silently adding the word "physically." I swallowed a blob of tuna sandwich that was stuck in my throat and drank some more water. Then I wiped my mouth with a napkin. "But you know what? Right this minute I'm really just wondering why they put onions in the tuna. And also too much mayo; it's kind of disgusting."

"Zinny," Kailani said quietly.

"You want to hear something funny? When I was little, I named my best Barbie 'Mayonnaise.' I thought it was the fanciest name ever, kind of French, or something."

Kailani and Maisie looked at each other.

"I had another Barbie named Salsa," I continued. "And Ken was Ketchup. I called him Ketch for short. That's definitely a boy name, don't you think? 'Hey, Ketch, sup?'"

"*Zinny,*" Kailani said. She wasn't smiling. "Why do you keep changing the subject?"

"What subject? You mean there's *only one* subject to ever talk about?"

"Hey, we can talk about whatever you want," Maisie

said sharply. "Including *serious things*, okay? *Real* things. That's *exactly* what we're trying to tell you!"

"Great! Then let's talk about how to identify poisonous mushrooms! Or how to escape a boa constrictor! Those are definitely real things!"

They were both staring at me.

"Or How to Survive Quicksand," I added.

Kailani rolled her eyes. "Okay, Zinny, *that's* not a real thing," she said.

Later the Same Day

When I got home that afternoon, Mom was in her bedroom with the door shut, arguing with someone on the phone about Gabriel's medical bills. Scarlett was in our bedroom, typing, and Aiden was at the dining room table, surrounded by his color-coded notebooks, a juice box, and a half-eaten bag of Goldfish crackers. As soon as he saw me, he pushed the crackers away, like he thought I'd scold him for spoiling his supper.

Except what supper would that be, anyway? I quickly scanned the kitchen. Mom hadn't left anything on the stove; there were no cooking smells coming from the oven.

Actually, I couldn't remember the last time she'd cooked a real, whole meal for the family instead of just scrambling eggs or making a pot of spaghetti or microwaving some Stouffer's. I didn't blame her for not cooking; I knew she was working all the time on Gabriel's stuff. But it kind of felt like she'd forgotten about the rest of us. And maybe also about herself.

As for Dad, he never cooked anyway. And actually, he'd been missing most suppers lately. Which had hardly ever happened before Gabriel's accident.

"Where's Mom?" Aiden asked, looking over my shoulder.

"On the phone," I said. "Wanna help me make supper?"

"You?" His forehead puckered. "But you can't cook, Zinny."

"Who says? It's not brain surgery, Aiden."

I opened the refrigerator and started collecting food specimens: a flabby carrot, some sprouting potatoes, a mushy onion, a lemon, a chunk of cheddar cheese, ketchup, hickory-smoke-flavor barbecue sauce, and an opened carton of organic low-sodium chicken stock. In the pantry closet I found a can of tuna, a can of chickpeas, and some pasta shaped like tennis rackets.

Most of it from Before the Accident, probably.

I chopped up the carrot, the potatoes, the onion, and

the cheese. Then I dumped everything in a big red enamel pot Mom only ever used for making chili. Gabriel's favorite. *Maybe she won't want to make it again,* I thought. *Until Gabriel comes home, whenever that is.*

Well, so this will taste the opposite of chili.

I looked inside the cupboard where Mom kept the spices and dried herbs. But all the jars looked really old. And to be honest, I didn't know what any of the flavors were, or what I was supposed to do with them.

I shut the cupboard door.

"What are we cooking?" Aiden asked.

"Tuna surprise," I heard myself say.

Aiden looked worried. "Is that a real thing? I always thought tuna surprise was made up."

"All recipes are made up."

"No, I mean, made up like a joke."

"Nah, tuna surprise is definitely a thing. I'm sure I've eaten it once or twice."

"But don't we need a recipe, Zinny? Maybe we could look it up online—"

"What for? We'll just use whatever we have. It'll be our own special family recipe. Besides, Aiden, where's your spirit of adventure?"

I wiggled my fingers in a mad-scientist sort of way.

At last Aiden smiled.

Third grade boys aren't exactly mysterious, I thought. *Good thing I totally get his sense of humor.*

I turned on the burner to medium, handed Aiden a big metal spoon, and told him to "stir until boiling."

"What happens then?" he asked.

"It cooks. So how's that big project going?"

"What big project?"

"You know. That thing you were telling me about before winter break. How to Survive When You Accidentally Shampoo Your Hair with Elmer's Glue."

"That wasn't the topic, Zinny." He stopped stirring. "And it's not due for a long, long time, We're just Conducting Research and Developing Our Ideas right now. Anyhow, I switched."

"You're not doing the quicksand thing? So what are you doing, then?"

"It doesn't matter."

"Of course it matters! And don't think you're not going to tell me, because I *demand* information."

He began stirring again. "How to Survive an Invasion of Cyborg Mosquitoes."

"Huh," I said, adding some salt to the pot. "Interesting. How are cyborg mosquitoes different from real ones?"

"They're programmed to attack people who itch the most."

"But if they're programmed, they can be hacked, right?" I argued. "So actually, they're not as invincible as the regular kind."

"Yeah, but the cyborg ones don't care about bug spray." He thought. "Also, bats don't eat the cyborg kind, so they have no natural predators."

"Well, *that* sucks. So how *do* you survive them, then?"

"You use light sabers to zap them. They're allergic to the vibrations." He held up his stirring spoon and made it shiver like a light saber.

"Gotcha," I said. "Cool topic, Aidy. Did you read about it somewhere?"

"Nah. I made it up."

"Well, I bet your class will love it. Hey, is the pot boiling yet?"

"No, but I see teeny bubbles."

"Keep stirring. Ms. Molina taught us about this when we did a chemistry unit—stirring speeds up the molecules to make them boil faster."

"Really?"

"Yep. You know, cooking is basically just chemistry—"

"What's that smell?" Now Scarlett was standing in the kitchen, her face scrunched up. "You guys are making supper?"

"Well, *somebody* has to," I said. "Mom's on the phone doing medical stuff for Gabriel. In her bedroom, with the door shut."

"So how do you know what she's doing?"

"Because I heard her though the door."

Scarlett frowned. "She didn't say anything about food?"

"Nope. She didn't even come out to say hello."

"Whoa," Scarlett said. "Mom *really* needs to start taking care of things again. And herself. I'm getting worried about her."

Scarlett made it sound like she was the only one worried. I almost said so, but I didn't want to start an argument in front of Aiden.

"*And* it would be nice if Dad came home for supper once in a while, instead of hiding at the office." Scarlett loomed over the pot. "No offense, but I'm not eating whatever this is supposed to be."

"It's tuna surprise," Aiden announced.

"Seriously? I always thought that was a joke."

"See?" Aiden told me.

"I'm sure it's delicious," I said. "Full of protein. And if you don't want any, Scar, more for the rest of us."

Scarlett made a barf face. "Hate to break it to you, Zin, but *no one* is eating this. Why don't we just order a pizza?"

"Could we?" Aiden begged her. "Please?"

The little traitor.

"Do what you want, guys," I said in an airy way. "*I'm* having tuna surprise. And I bet Mom and Dad will at least *try* it."

"Hey, Zinny, don't guilt them, okay? They're dealing with enough." Scarlett flashed her eyes at me, like the two of us were keeping a secret from Aiden, which we obviously weren't.

I glared back.

"Anyway," Scarlett continued, "I'm sure it tastes like year-old sewage."

That did it. I grabbed the spoon from Aiden's hand, dipped it in the sauce, blew on the hot liquid, and sipped. At first it was sweet and tomatoey. But a second later it fizzed on my tongue in an alarming way. *Yeow,* I thought. *Maybe that chicken stock was older than I thought.*

I dumped the whole thing down the sink.

Then I poked Aiden with the spoon. "Hey, here's a topic: How to Survive Tuna Surprise," I murmured, making my eyebrows go all Evil Mastermind.

He yelped out a laugh.

Scarlett, who was phoning in the pizza order, frowned at us to be quiet.

The Next Day

I knocked on the door of the lab.

"Oh, hi, Zinny!" Ms. Molina's eyes were bright behind her black glasses, and her thick brown hair flopped over her shoulder. She was the sort of person who always looked pretty even though she didn't care about looking pretty. At least, that was how it seemed to me.

"Done with lunch already?" she asked, smiling.

"Actually, I wasn't hungry," I said.

"You didn't go to lunch?"

I shook my head. Lunch meant sitting with Kailani and Maisie. And that meant:

1) Talking about James Ramos, or

2) Specifically not talking about James Ramos, or

3) Talking about Gabriel, or

4) Talking about why we weren't talking about Gabriel.

The truth was, I couldn't deal with any of those options. That morning Maisie, Kailani, and I had walked to school like always. And though they'd chatted the whole time about some web show they were both watching, I couldn't stop reading their thought balloons: *See, Zinny? Look at us! We're not asking about your brother, and we're even having a non-James Ramos conversation! Woohoo!*

But now Ms. Molina was frowning at me. "Well, you should definitely eat *something*, Zinny. If you're hungry later, you won't pay good attention in class."

"Oh, don't worry, I will," I protested. "I always pay attention in science. It's my favorite subject."

"I had a feeling." She handed me what was left of her sandwich. "Almond butter and banana on semolina," she explained. "You're not allergic to nuts? Or gluten?"

I shook my head. "But really, you don't have to—"

"That's okay, I'm stuffed. Today is Mr. Patrick's birthday. Have you ever chatted with him?"

I shook my head. Mr. Patrick was a new guidance counselor. He had a semi-bald head and wore a lot of flannel shirts. But that was all I knew about him.

"Well, he's really nice," Ms. Molina said. "And today's his birthday, so he brought in a birthday cake for the teachers' lounge. Of course, I had a huge slice just to be polite, and also because, you know, *chocolate*." She grinned. "Hey, wanna see something?"

She beckoned me over to her laptop. On the screen was a photo of a fuzzy yellow spider. "My dream pet. Maybe not for the classroom, though, because they're nocturnal."

"Your dream pet is a *bug*?"

She laughed. "It's not a 'bug,' Zinny. It's a Rio Grande gold tarantula from Texas. They're completely docile, but they'll bite you in self-defense. The venom's not poisonous, though. Isn't she gorgeous?"

Use "they" if you're not sure of the gender. I chewed on the sandwich. "How do you know it's a she?"

"Oh, because the females are bigger than the males. And listen to the scientific name: *Aphonopelma moderatum*. Don't you just love the ring of that?"

One of my favorite things about Ms. Molina was how much she cared about scientific names for things. Like she believed that if you just knew the right words, you could unlock a whole treasure box of information. I wondered if all scientists felt the way Ms. Molina did. It was comforting to think about, really.

Ms. Molina was smiling at me as I swallowed a blob of banana. "So, Zinny. Are you excited about our upcoming animal study?" she asked.

"I didn't know we were doing one," I admitted.

"Oh yes! It's the best part of the seventh grade curriculum. Actual animal guests in our classroom! In their own special tanks! Of course, I can't reveal their identity quite yet. But soon." She closed out of the tarantula page. "So. Anything else I can do for you today?"

I blushed. Ms. Molina had never asked that question before; she'd always just let me hang out with her. But maybe I'd blown it today by showing up at the start of lunch period. Also stealing her sandwich.

As I watched her lean over her sunny windowsill to examine a weird-looking cactus she was growing, my brain scrambled for a reason to be there.

"Actually, I was thinking about herbs," I blurted.

She turned to me with raised eyebrows.

"I'm thinking of planting a few," I said quickly. "By our

house. And I mean, if it's not convenient for you, or you don't know about them, I could just look them up online. But I thought maybe, since you're so into plants and everything—"

By now I was feeling completely stupid. Why was I bothering her with this?

But Ms. Molina just nodded. "Well, to be honest, Zinny, I've never grown any herbs before. I'm actually more of a cacti-and-succulents person. But I'd love to learn about them with you. May I ask why the interest?"

"I don't know. Spring is coming pretty soon, right? And the weather's been so warm lately. And rainy. So I thought my mom and I . . . maybe we could grow some herbs. And use them for cooking together. As a sort of project."

As I said this, I imagined Ms. Molina's thought balloon: *A project with her mom? Oh, of course—that's obviously about her brother.*

But if Ms. Molina was thinking this, that wasn't what she said. "What a lovely idea. I'd be delighted to help. Tell me about your garden."

"We don't have one. We used to, but this year, my mom's been really busy . . ." I couldn't finish.

Ms. Molina started typing into her laptop again. "What's your exposure?"

"Excuse me?"

"Which way does your house face? North, south . . ."

"I'm not sure."

"Okay." She smiled patiently. "Do you get morning sun or afternoon?"

"Afternoon. Except when it's raining."

"Yes, Zinny, that's the norm: no sun when it's raining. Although it's not strict scientific law."

I blushed again. She was teasing me, but in a nice, teachery sort of way.

About twenty minutes later, we had a list of herbs to try growing: thyme, bay, sage, rosemary, lavender. Ideally, we should wait a month or so, Ms. Molina said; but if the weather stayed warm over the next few weeks, we could try to plant early, because these herbs were all hardy. Ms. Molina said she'd talk to her tia Marisol, who owned a plant nursery, and let me know which were in stock. ("Don't worry, she always gives me the niece discount," Ms. Molina said, winking.)

She also printed out a list of the scientific names, which I recited to myself the rest of the afternoon. A sort of song, or maybe a kind of chant: *Laurus nobilis. Thymus vulgaris. Salvia officinalis. Salvia rosmarinus. Lavandula, lavandula, lavandula.*

Late January

About three weeks after Gabriel arrived at Redwoods Village, they said the whole family was allowed to visit. I say "allowed" because they didn't let us come before then, for reasons I didn't understand and Scarlett was convinced were against the law.

"He's not *in jail*," she kept saying. "He didn't commit a *crime*. And they have no business stealing his phone!"

"They didn't steal it, sweetheart," Dad said. "They'll give it back when they think he's ready."

"They just want him in a good place," Mom said.

"Yeah?" Scarlett snapped. "Then he shouldn't be *there*.

Redwood Town, or whatever they're calling it."

"Redwoods Village," Mom corrected her. "I mean in a good place mentally. Stable. And ready for a productive family visit."

Productive family visit. Since when did family visits need to be "productive"?

We drove up there on a Friday night. It was a two-hour trip, and by the time we arrived at the motel, Mom said it was too late to see Gabriel, so we'd meet him in the morning for breakfast.

"Can we go to IHOP?" Aiden begged.

"No, sweetheart. We'll eat with him in the dining hall. Then Dad and I have a therapy session with Gabe and his doctor."

Scarlett and I locked eyes. So this was what Mom meant by "productive family visit." It wasn't going to be normal at all.

"Ugh, I wish I hadn't come," Scarlett murmured. And I didn't even tell her not to say it.

The next morning at exactly nine o'clock, we arrived at the Redwoods Village dining hall. It was a large room with big windows and exposed beams, the kind that are supposed to look cabin-y and cozy. But the dining hall still had the loud, clattery sound of a school lunchroom, and the same sort of chemical smell, like it had just been sprayed with Lysol.

"Isn't this nice?" Dad exclaimed. It was a bright, cheery voice I hadn't heard in a long time; I couldn't help feeling he'd kept it from us, hidden away. Almost like he thought the rest of us didn't deserve it or something. But right away I was sorry that I had this idea.

I watched Dad's face light up as he looked across the dining hall. "Oh hey—is that Gabe?"

Mom made a small sound like a trapped bird. Then she ran across the dining room to where Gabriel was sitting by himself. She threw her arms around him and hugged.

The rest of us followed quickly.

Gabriel stood and hugged us one by one. His hair was long and stringy and he still looked thin and pale, although maybe not as flattened as he'd seemed back at home. Which was just a few weeks ago—although really, with Abnormal Standard Time, how could you be sure?

For a long, weird moment we all just stared at him. Kind of like he was one of Ms. Molina's creatures in a small glass tank, I thought.

"So, is anybody hungry?" Dad finally said in the same bright, cheery voice.

"Me!" Aiden shouted.

We grabbed trays and food—we kids had pancakes, Mom had a toasted bagel, and Dad had scrambled eggs and bacon.

"This is way better than IHOP," Aiden said through a mouthful of pancake.

"Yeah, except it's not the normal breakfast around here," Gabriel said. He even smiled at Aiden, although his eyes were tired. "This is visitor food."

"But meals are okay generally?" Mom asked.

Gabriel shrugged. "I'd rather eat anywhere else. *Be* anywhere else. To be perfectly honest."

Scarlett's eyes met mine.

We talked about random things as we ate—the Golden State Warriors (Gabriel's favorite basketball team), how to order Gabriel some new sneakers. Then Dad announced it was time for their therapy session. So Scarlett, Aiden, and I could walk the grounds, or "park ourselves" in the recreation room "for a bit." And afterward, Dad said eagerly, maybe Gabriel could take us for a tour? We could all see his room, and Dad had been wanting to check out the rock wall and the ropes course. And maybe also the aquatics center—

"Dad, it's not college," Gabriel grumbled.

The too-bright light went out of Dad's eyes. "Yes, I know that, Gabe," he said.

Scarlett looked at me again.

Scarlett, Aiden, and I walked around the main building twice; then Scarlett complained her shoes were pinching. So we came back inside and wandered the first floor, past the mindfulness room, the arts center, and a door labeled MASSAGE / ACUPUNCTURE / SALON. By then I had the feeling that Redwoods Village was a lot less fancy than all these signs on the doors suggested. And anyway, it wasn't a village at all, just four box-shaped buildings in the middle of nowhere, with an actual redwood forest twenty miles away.

Finally we found the indoor recreation center, which was basically a room with an old GameCube, a Ping-Pong table, and shelves with moldy-looking board games. Two teen girls were playing one of the Mario Kart games. I wondered if they had what Gabriel did—bipolar disorder. You couldn't tell just by looking.

Aiden made me play Ping-Pong with him while Scarlett

read her phone. After a while Aiden said he wanted to watch the video game, so Scarlett and I started playing Scrabble.

Once when it was her turn, Scarlett coughed a few times. When Aiden didn't turn around, she leaned across the board and spoke to me in a quiet voice. "Oh, by the way, Zinny. I wanted to tell you something. I'm seeing a therapist."

"You are?"

"Uh-huh. Mom made me. But I told her I'd see somebody only if *she* did too."

I stared at my sister. "You told *Mom* she should see a *therapist*?"

"*Shh,*" Scarlett said. "Well, yeah. Considering how stressed she's been since Gabriel's accident, I think that's a good idea, don't you?"

I nodded. But I couldn't stop myself from thinking: Weren't we supposed to *not* talk about Gabriel? To anyone, especially total strangers? Mom was the one who'd told us that, so it seemed weird for Scarlett to tell *her* to talk to somebody. And even weirder that Mom would listen.

Although probably therapists didn't count as "total strangers."

"Anyway," Scarlett was saying, "Mom knew a social

worker through her school, and I saw her on Thursday. She's pretty nice, actually. Her name is Elyse."

I chewed my lip. *Why is Scarlett telling me this right now? Why* here? *Does she think she's going crazy too?*

Maybe we all are. Including Mom. Including Dad.

And if that's true, would talking about it even help?

"Your turn, Zinny," Scarlett said, poking my arm.

I made the word SECRET.

After way longer than "a bit," Mom, Dad, and Gabriel showed up, looking exhausted. Mom's eyes were red, and she was sniffling into a damp-looking tissue.

"How was your session?" Scarlett asked.

"Good," Dad said. His voice was quiet. Back to the way he sounded most of the time these days. "Helpful, I think."

"Oh, definitely," Mom said, wiping her nose.

I searched Gabriel's face, but there weren't any clues.

"Wanna play Ping-Pong, Gabriel?" Aiden asked him. "I beat Zinny eleven times."

"And I beat you fifteen," I reminded him.

Gabriel reached over and mussed Aiden's hair. "No offense, buddy. I'm really glad to see you all and everything, but right now I just want to rest."

"That's fine," Mom said quickly. "Of course, sweet-heart."

"The meds make you tired?" Dad asked.

"A little. Less than they did at first. Anyway." Suddenly Gabriel threw his arms around me. "I'm glad you came, Monkeygirl."

"Me too," I managed to say.

He hugged Aiden, then Scarlett.

"You need to get out of here," Scarlett told him.

"I'm trying," Gabriel said.

The whole drive home, the five of us barely talked. And when Scarlett and I were back in our bedroom, she slammed the door behind us.

"Well, that's the last time I'm visiting *that* place," she said.

Six Years Before, Early Saturday Morning

The scene: Gabriel (age twelve), Scarlett (age ten), Aiden (age two), and me (age six) are all smooshed together on the TV room sofa. Gabriel has the remote set on mute as we watch the worst show ever on Cartoon Network: My Dog, Drools. Gabriel does the voice for Captain Bob, because he's the oldest. Scarlett does his wisecracking sidekick, Taffy. I'm the house robot, Click. And Aiden, who doesn't talk much yet, is Drools.

GABRIEL: *Hey, that looks like a haunted house! We should totally sneak inside and explore it without any weapons or reinforcements.*

SCARLETT: *Not me, Captain Bob. I have an important dentist appointment.*

GABRIEL: *Who cares about your one-eyed dentist, Taffy? There could be ghosts in that spooky attic! And zombies! And brain-eating amoebas!*

ME: *Gabriel, don't say that.*

SCARLETT: *He's only kidding, Zinny.*

ME: *Okay. But I'm not playing if he says that.*

GABRIEL: *Delete that! There are definitely no brain-eating amoebas in that haunted house, Taffy! But wait, who's that behind us? With the laser pointer?*

SCARLETT: *It's only a firefly, Captain Bob.*

GABRIEL: *Not in the middle of the day! It's got to be an alien adversary of unknown origin! Let's ask Click to identify it for us! (Pokes me.)*

ME *(robot voice): Meep. Beep. One thousand twenty-three million.*

GABRIEL: *Exactly as I thought, Taffy! Click is saying the alien is from the planet Zeerocks! And it's here to turn us all into tofu!*

SCARLETT: *Oh no! I hate tofu! It tastes like a soapy dishwashing sponge! There's only one hope!*

GABRIEL: *Exactly! We must get Drools to neutralize the alien with super-slobber!*

ME: *What's "neutralize" mean?*

SCARLETT: *"Turn off." Shh, Zinny.*

ME: *Okay. But no killing!*

GABRIEL: *Drools, go ahead! SLOBBER ATTACK!*

AIDEN: *(climbs off sofa, crawls around TV room making slobbery mouth noises)*

GABRIEL: *Good work, Drools! Here's a bone for you as a reward. But wait! The zombies have captured me! And now I can't—smffrff!*

SCARLETT: *Don't worry, Captain Bob! We'll save you!*

ME: *The zombies got him?*

SCARLETT *(ignoring me): We'll defeat them with my magic flyswatter! Drools, what are you saying? No flyswatter?*

AIDEN: *Arf, arf!*

SCARLETT: *Well, okay, Drools, if you insist. Run into the haunted house to save Captain Bob from the zombies! But don't slobber on the sofa! And be careful!*

Middle of February

Aiden's class took a trip to the Natural History Museum, so he was late getting home that day. I knew he'd be late—his teacher had sent a note explaining the schedule—but even so, when I got home from school and he wasn't at the dining room table with his juice box and all his notebooks spread out, my heart started to skip a little.

I scolded myself: *Don't freak out! People are allowed to be late! It doesn't mean something terrible happened!*

But still, I couldn't focus on my homework, or on anything else. I just kept chewing my lip until it felt sore, then smeared on some cherry ChapStick. And the way Mom was pacing around the living room, peeking out the curtain every five minutes, I could tell she was starting to freak too.

Finally, we heard the doorbell: *bling blang.* Mom and I both ran to the front door. There was Aiden (looking a bit carsick, I thought), along with Rudy and Rudy's nosy mom, Mrs. Halloran.

"Returning your package," Mrs. Halloran said, laughing as if she'd cracked the most hilarious joke in the world. "Aiden had a great time. Didn't you, honey?"

Aiden nodded. "Yeah, we saw an a-pat-o-SAUR-us."

"You mean a-PAT-osaurus," Rudy corrected him, rolling his eyes.

"Aiden's right, actually," I said.

Rudy shrugged in a snotty way. "Nah," he told me. "I know *all about* dinosaurs. *And* how to pronounce them."

Rudy's mom beamed. "Yes, Rudy's obsessed with paleontology; I keep telling myself it's not a problem! Anyway, Aiden was very well-behaved on the class trip. It was a pleasure being assigned to supervise him."

Well-behaved. Supervise. A-PAT-osaurus. I narrowed my eyes at both of them.

"Well, Rosa, thanks for bringing Aiden home," Mom said lamely.

"No problem." Suddenly Mrs. Halloran grabbed Mom's hand. "So how is Gabriel doing?" she asked in a voice dripping with concern.

"Oh, he's doing very well, thanks," Mom replied. "All healed up now. Back in school, and working hard!"

Wait, what?

I stared at Mom, who was doing a stiff little fake smile.

And I felt this in my stomach: She wasn't "protecting Gabriel's privacy"; she was *lying*. Adding details, pretending Gabriel was back in college, "doing very well" and "working hard." Why would Mom lie about Gabriel? Was she ashamed that her own kid was crazy?

Really, I couldn't think of any other reason.

Two Days Later, in Morning Homeroom

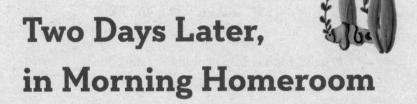

On Wednesday, my homeroom teacher handed me a sealed blue envelope. *ZINNIA MANNING*, it said in green ink, all caps.

"What's that?" Maisie asked immediately. "It looks like an invitation. You should open it, Zinny."

Did she think I wouldn't? And that I needed her to tell me that?

I carefully unsealed the envelope and took out a pale blue notecard. With Maisie and Kailani looking over my shoulder, I unfolded it to read more green ink:

Dear Zinnia,

You are invited to join today's Lunch Club in Mr. Patrick's room (107B). We all look forward to seeing you there!

Welcome!

Mr. Patrick, Luz, Jayden, Keira, and Asher

"Oh, ugh," Maisie said behind her hand.

I looked at her. "Why do you say that?"

She leaned closer. "Zinny, it sounds like one of those awful guidance groups, where they make you sit in a circle and do bonding exercises. My sister was stuck in a group like that the year she had no friends; I *know* it's the kind of thing you'd *hate*. And those other kids . . ." She made a barf face.

I nodded. I didn't know any Luz or Jayden, which probably meant they were eighth graders. But Asher Hyland was a seventh grader; he was famous at school for being weird. And the only thing I knew about Keira Jacobson was that she was always getting into fights with people. Why did Mr. Patrick think I needed to hang out with kids like *that*?

"Maybe you don't have to do it," Maisie said. "I mean, it's just an invitation, right?"

I reread the green words. *You are invited to join.* Like

this "Lunch Club" was some sort of special honor.

"I guess I could say no thanks," I said. "I mean, it's just an invitation."

"Although it could be not *so* bad," Kailani said softly.

Maisie bug-eyed her. "Are you serious, Kailani? Those guidance groups are like *torture*."

"I don't know. If it's a lunch club, they probably have food." Kailani shrugged.

"Who cares about *food*?" Maisie demanded. "The point is that Zinny needs lunchtime to be with her *friends*! Mr. Patrick is a guidance counselor, so he should understand that, right?"

What she said made my cheeks burn. After the almond-butter-and-banana sandwich lunch, I'd been afraid to go back to see Ms. Molina, because I didn't want to be all, *So? Did you get my herbs yet?* But my plan was to go to the lab today. *Not* eat in the lunchroom with Maisie and Kailani.

Then I remembered how Ms. Molina had eaten a slice of Mr. Patrick's birthday cake. Which didn't mean they were friends or anything, but it did mean they talked to each other. For all I knew, they'd planned this "invitation" together. A tiny part of me wondered if it was Ms. Molina's idea. *Zinny's been hanging out with me a little too much lately.*

Know any weirdo kids she could sit in a room with during lunch period?

"Just don't go," Maisie told me. "No one's forcing you to do it. And what could happen if you don't?"

"I guess I'll find out," I said, tossing the envelope and the blue notecard in the trash.

When Gabriel gets his driving license, he wants to see how far he can drive Mom's car on an empty tank. Just out of curiosity, he says. So when the fuel gauge flashes Empty, he doesn't get gasoline. And when the car stops moving halfway down the hill on Baker Street, he calls Dad at work, who doesn't think it's funny. At all.

"Gabriel, what was the point of that experiment?" he shouts at my brother when they finally get home.

"I just wanted to see what would happen," Gabriel says.

"Yeah? Well, let me tell you what happened." Dad crosses his arms on his chest. "You pulled me out of an important meeting. We wasted an hour waiting for the garage to bring gas. And let's not forget the most important detail here: you put yourself in danger by driving a car that wasn't functioning." Dad shakes his head. "Gabriel, you're a smart kid. But explain this—you thought the refill-the-gas-tank rule just didn't apply to you?"

•

Gabriel never answered that question.

Because really, what could he say? It was such a dumb and dangerous thing to do. And so inconsiderate of everybody else.

Was I like my brother that way? Did I think some things just didn't apply to me—like Mr. Patrick's "invitation," for example?

The question made my heart bang, and gave me a strange, cold, sweaty feeling all morning.

Same Day, Fourth Period

By fourth-period math, I'd changed my mind about Lunch Club. My reasoning was this: Even if Ms. Molina hadn't arranged the whole thing, I knew that if I ignored the "invitation," she'd hear about it in the teachers' room, either directly from Mr. Patrick or over some other teacher's birthday cake. Then maybe the next time I showed up at her lab during lunch, she'd chase me away. And I desperately needed to hang out with her and see photos of tarantulas.

Besides, I told myself, I only needed to go once. I could show up in Mr. Patrick's room fifth period, be polite, smile at everyone, and never go back. The invitation had said

You are invited to join today's *Lunch Club,* not *You are invited to join Lunch Club from now until you lose all your grown-up teeth.* I wouldn't just ignore the blue notecard; I'd keep everyone (except my friends) happy.

Of course, I didn't explain this to Maisie and Kailani. Because they wouldn't understand—not the refill-the-gas-tank rule, not Gabriel's behavior, not the Ms. Molina part, none of it.

Same Day, Lunch Period

The scene: Room 107B. Door is open. Girl is sitting on a lumpy-looking red couch. She has warm brown skin, dark hair piled on top of her head in a messy bun, and dimples.

GIRL: You here for the group?

ME *(smearing lips with cherry ChapStick)*: Well, yes. If you mean the Lunch Club.

GIRL *(laughing a little)*: Lunch Club? No one calls it that but Mr. Patrick.

ME: Really? What do you call it, then?

GIRL: Ralph.

ME *(thought balloon)*: *She's joking, right?*

(Extremely cute, tall, skinny, Black boy with curly eyelashes, and small pale girl with frizzy brown hair and green glasses enter the room. I know who this girl is: Keira. They plop on the couch next to Girl, and greet one another warmly.)

GIRL *(to me)*: So I'm Luz. This is Jayden and Keira.

JAYDEN *(swats her on the arm)*: We can introduce ourselves. Luz thinks she runs this thing.

LUZ *(swats him back)*: I do not. So who are you?

ME: Me? Um, Zinnia.

JAYDEN *(grins)*: Umzinnia is a funny name.

ME *(trying not to stare at him. Because he is* cute. *Way cuter than James Ramos)*: No, not Umzinnia. Just Zinnia, like the flower. But you can call me Zinny. Or Zin.

(Asher enters—an olive-skinned boy with messy dark brown hair in his face. He slumps into the metal chair next to me, his arms folded across his chest. He stares at the floor tiles.)

LUZ: I like that better. Zin.

JAYDEN: Yeah, but it's *her* name. So *she* gets to decide what we call her, not you.

LUZ: I *know* that, you fool. I'm just voicing my honest opinion. Hey, Asher. How's it going?

ASHER: *(grunting noise)*

JAYDEN: Yeah, me too.

(Door opens. Mr. Patrick enters, wearing a green flannel shirt and khakis with baggy knees.

MR. PATRICK *(extending his hand to shake mine)*: Zinnia?

LUZ: *Zin.*

ME: Or Zinny. Whatever.

MR. PATRICK: Well, we're very glad to welcome you, Zinny. I'm Mr. Patrick. Have people been introducing themselves?

LUZ: Keira hasn't. And neither has Asher.

KEIRA: Maybe we would if you'd stop talking, Luz. Anyhow, Zinny already knows who I am.

MR. PATRICK *(swivels desk chair to sit beside Asher, rubs hands, leans forward)*: So this week I ordered one pepperoni, one plain. Everyone approve?

JAYDEN: Yeah.

LUZ: I approve, but next time can we *please* get mushroom?

KEIRA: Only *you* like mushroom, Luz.

LUZ: Yes, but I don't like it. I *love* it.

KEIRA: Then bring your own and add it to the plain.

LUZ: Oh, great, Keira. You want me to sauté some mushrooms at home and bring them to school every week in a little sandwich bag? That will just get all smashed up inside my backpack?

KEIRA: Hey, I'm not telling you *how* to bring them. I'm just saying since *you're* the only one who eats mushroom—

MR. PATRICK *(interrupting)*: The pizza will be here in a few minutes, guys, so why don't we get started. Anybody want to get the ball rolling?

LUZ: I will. So my mom? She, like, totally lost it on Saturday because I was with my friends and forgot to tell her I'd be fifteen minutes late. She went *insane* on me, I swear. And then my dad was like, "Don't you ever, *ever* do that to your mother again, you hear me, Luz?" Like I did it *to* her.

MR. PATRICK: That must have been tough to deal with, Luz. Why do you think your mom reacted that way?

LUZ: Because she's crazy.

JAYDEN: She isn't crazy. She's just worried about you.

LUZ: Yeah, but *I* don't give her anything to worry about. *Ever.* So it's totally unfair she's taking it out on me.

MR. PATRICK: Taking what out on you?

LUZ: You know. The whole thing with my sister. Grief.

ME *(panicky thought balloon)*: *Wait a minute. Did she just say "grief"? Is that what this club is about? Because if it is—*

KEIRA: Yeah, my mom is exactly the same. Ever since my dad left, it's like she thinks *I'm* divorcing her too. "What time will you be home? Where will you be in the next five minutes?" She does it to my sister Jocelyn, too, who's in high school, so she, like, freaks.

LUZ: Right? Omigod. It's so embarrassing! *(Turns to me.)* Does your mom check up on you all the time, Zin?

ME: Mine? No, not really. And my parents aren't divorced, so.

KEIRA: You're lucky, then. It sucks.

ME *(confused thought balloon)*: *So I guess this is the Grief and Divorce Club? Maybe?*

(Long, uncomfortable pause.)

MR. PATRICK: So how's your dad doing, Jayden?

JAYDEN: Pretty good. On Saturday he played basketball with my brother and me. For almost an hour. First time since he got sick.

ME *(even more confused thought balloon)*: *Okay . . . the Grief and Divorce and Sick Dad Club? Not sure I see where this is heading . . .*

LUZ *(smacks Jayden's arm)*: What? Why didn't you tell me?

JAYDEN: I was saving it.

LUZ: Dude, I need to *hear* happy stuff like that.

KEIRA: So do I. Don't keep it to yourself, Jayden! That's just mean!

JAYDEN *(beams)*: Sorry.

MR. PATRICK: Well, that's wonderful news, Jayden. Did you guys keep score?

JAYDEN: Nah. But I made two three-pointers. And Dad had a slam dunk.

MR. PATRICK *(fist-bumps Jayden)*: Nice. What about you, Asher?

ASHER: What about me *what*?

LUZ: Hey, that's rude!

MR. PATRICK: It's okay, Luz. We were just wondering how things are going, Asher.

ASHER *(shrugs)*: Same.

MR. PATRICK: Okay. Want to share anything?

ASHER: If I felt like "sharing," I would.

MR. PATRICK: Got it. Well, maybe next time.

ASHER: Yeah, maybe. Maybe not.

(Another pause.)

(Pause still going.)

(Still going.)

(Yep. Still going.)

ME: *(sound of heart beating)*

MR. PATRICK: Zinny, how about you?

ME *(fidgets with super-tiny-chair charm in hoodie pocket)*: Me?

LUZ: Come on, we won't bite.

KEIRA: And if we do, it's not poisonous. Usually.

LUZ: *Never.* Shut up, Keira. *(Slaps her arm playfully.)*

ME: Um. Well, actually, I'm not sure I want to do this . . . club, or whatever it is. Actually. But, um, thanks for inviting me today.

LUZ *(pouts)*: You don't like us?

ME: No, no. I just don't—I don't know. Need to do this. Sorry.

KEIRA: Nobody ever thinks they need to do this.

LUZ: Yeah, well, *I* do.

KEIRA: Okay, Luz, but you're weird. Anyway, two kids dropped out last month, didn't they?

MR. PATRICK: And they're always welcome back, Keira. So are you, Zinny, anytime. Lunch Club is just about being here for each other while we're going through some challenging stuff in our lives. It's okay to just show up and enjoy a slice of pizza.

JAYDEN: Which is always really good, by the way. Much better than the cafeteria.

KEIRA: Yeah, *much.* Even the plain.

MR. PATRICK: And, Zinny, if you *do* choose to share with us, you should know nothing leaves this room.

LUZ: Right. Because it's classified information! And we all have top-level security clearance.

JAYDEN: Ha.

LUZ: Well, *I* do, anyway. And so does Asher, but he'll never confess. Oh, and also we have a secret handshake.

JAYDEN *(laughing)*: We do? What is it?

LUZ *(mysterious voice)*: Zinny has to tune in next episode to find out.

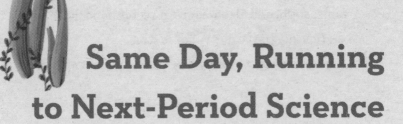

Same Day, Running to Next-Period Science

Well, that was awkward.

But I did it.

Once.

And now I never have to do it again

Even if they invite me.

Which they probably won't—

I mean, it was pretty clear that I didn't
    want to be there.

Not that they did either, obviously.

Because really

Mr. Patrick could serve the best pizza—

My Life in the Fish Tank

All the toppings just the way you like
   them
(Or no toppings at all)
A perfect thin crust
Fresh tomato sauce
And extra cheese—
But still
No one wants to be in a club like that.

Same Day, Science Class

At the start of science class Ms. Molina announced that she was ready to reveal which animal we'd be studying in our spring animal unit.

"Hey, I know, a vampire bat," guessed James Ramos. "Or a vampire."

"No, it's Sasquatch," said Darius Blade, a loud, spitty boy with too many freckles. "Or wait. How about an assassin vine?"

"What's that?" Aspen Garber asked. She looked worried.

"Assassin vines? They're these vines that trap animals and squeeze them to death like cobras. They have this poison fruit that looks like grapes—"

"*Stop,*" Ms. Molina said, smiling. "We're not experimenting with poisonous plants, Darius. And in case I need to remind anyone, this is science class, not science fiction. So no Sasquatch, and definitely no vampires."

On the whiteboard she wrote: *Cambarellus puer.*

"Any guesses?" she asked, smiling. "Zinnia?"

Everyone turned to look at me. How was *I* supposed to know this?

"I don't know," I said, blushing. "Maybe some type of cactus? Or succulent?"

"*Succulent,*" Darius repeated, like it was the funniest word in the world.

Ms. Molina ignored him. "Good guess, Zinny, but our subject is not a plant. Let me share a little more information."

Glancing at an index card, she wrote:

Kingdom: Animalia

Phylum: Arthropoda

Subphylum: Crustacea

Class: Malacostraca

Order: Decapoda

Family: Cambaridae

Genus: Cambarellus

Species: C. puer

Ms. Molina folded the index card and slipped it into the

pocket of her cardigan, like she was hiding the punchline of a joke. "All right, gang, let's not be afraid of these strange-looking words. A few of them should ring some bells."

"*Animalia* looks like animal," Aspen said.

Darius smacked his forehead.

Ms. Molina ignored him. "It certainly does," she said. "Any more ideas?"

"*Crustacea* looks like crustacean," I said. "So maybe . . . Are we doing lobsters? Or shrimp? Or crabs?"

Ms. Molina beamed. "A small cousin of theirs called the swamp dwarf crayfish. What can you infer about these creatures, based on what I wrote on the board?"

"Nothing," Darius said. "It's a weird foreign language."

"Scientific names are always in Latin," I said. "And *decapoda*—does that mean the creature has ten feet?"

"Bingo," Ms. Molina said, clicking on her computer. On the overhead monitor we could all see an image of what looked like a tiny brownish lobster.

"We're not *dissecting* those things, right?" Li-Mei Wen called out.

"No dissecting," Ms. Molina promised. "And no eating, either. We'll be observing their behavior in special fish tanks we'll get to design, and of course conducting experiments."

"Who'd want to eat crayfish, anyway?" Darius said, making a face.

"People eat crayfish all the time," Aspen said. "And, omigod, I love lobster. For my birthday? My grandma took me to this incredibly fancy restaurant that had the biggest ones ever. Like they each weighed over five pounds!"

If Kailani and Maisie had been in this class, we'd have been doing a group eye roll. No surprise that Aspen Garber went to a fancy restaurant for her birthday, where of course they had *the biggest lobsters ever*. She was such a braggy person, and so predictable.

Not that predictable was such a bad thing, I reminded myself.

In fact, the more I thought about it lately, "predictable" was pretty much a compliment.

After School
That Day

That day I decided to do a little grocery shopping after school. Because Scarlett was right: Mom still wasn't taking care of things. She'd started running again, which was definitely a good thing, but that meant that for big parts of every afternoon, she wasn't around. And she still wasn't doing much shopping or cooking. When Dad came home from work, often after supper, he usually just sat in the TV room by himself, watching basketball, even if it wasn't a team he cared about. On weekends he made himself sandwiches; he never asked what the rest of us were eating and barely said anything to us, really. Of the kids, Scarlett should have been the one stepping up to make dinner, clean the house, do grownup-ish things like that, but all she did after school was hang out online. And as far as she was concerned, pizza or Stouffer's for dinner every night was just fine.

So I stopped off at Ellman's Market, a little store a few blocks from our house, where we had an account. I bought some cut-up chicken parts, carrots, a handful of string beans, a can of chicken stock, rice, three apples, three bananas, a jar of peanut butter, a loaf of bread, a gallon of milk, a bag of Sun Chips, and a box of Oreos. Also a new cherry ChapStick for myself.

Maisie and Kailani came to help lug the groceries home in our backpacks. They didn't ask where I'd been at lunch, or why I was doing all this Mom work now; I guess they realized it was Gabriel-related, and that I didn't want to talk about it.

Phew. What a relief, I thought.

But then.

Just as we were finished putting away the groceries in the kitchen, Kailani turned to me. "So . . . how's your mom doing, Zinny?"

"Okay," I said, biting the edges off a Sun Chip.

"I haven't seen her in a long time. Is she home?"

"She's out running."

Maisie's eyes narrowed like she'd caught me lying. "You know, Zinny," she said, "my mom says she'd help you guys anytime."

"So would mine," Kailani said eagerly. "Anything you need, Zinny. Shopping, cooking, driving you places—"

"Thanks, that's really nice," I said. "But we're doing fine. Mom's getting back in shape—"

"Oh, come on, Zinny," Maisie exploded. "Why don't you ever tell us the truth?"

"About what?" My heart felt like a bowling ball falling down a flight of stairs.

"About *anything*. You weren't with Ms. Molina at lunch today."

"How do you know?" I stared. "You guys went *looking* for me?"

"Don't be mad," Kailani begged. "When you didn't show up in the lunchroom—"

"What did you think? That I ran away?"

"You went to that Lunch Club thing, right?" Maisie's voice was sharp, like an accusation.

"Maisie," I said, my voice growing as loud and sharp as

hers. "If I did, it was my choice. *My* choice. The Lunch Club is about *me*, not you. And if I *did* go, I didn't need your permission, okay?"

Maisie's pale face went pink. "All I *meant* was that we had a conversation about it, didn't we? In homeroom. And you acted like you weren't going. So then if you *did* go—"

"Well, I changed my mind. That's not allowed?"

"Well, sure! Of course it is! But why not just *tell* us that?"

Kailani's mouth got pinched. "Zinny, all we're saying is we don't know what's going on, because you never talk to us about anything. And every time we ask, you shut us down."

"Well, that's because it feels like you're watching me all the time! Waiting for me to cry, or fall apart, or something! Like I'm some kind of creature you're studying. In a fish tank!"

"A *fish tank*?" Maisie rolled her eyes. "Zinny, what are you even *talking* about?"

My heart was in my throat. I couldn't answer.

Now Kailani looked like she was about to cry. "All right, you guys, can we please, please change the subject?"

"Yeah, but to what?" Maisie challenged her. "Because Zinny acts like everything we say is dumb and boring."

"You mean James Ramos?" I said, my voice coming out

too loud and hoarse. "Because, frankly, James Ramos is like this brain-eating amoeba. If I have to listen to one more conversation about his stupid ears or his hair, I'll start drooling."

"Fine! Whatever!" Maisie was shouting now. "So if we're not allowed to talk about James, or about your brother, or your mom, *or* what's going on with *you*, what *are* we supposed to talk about?"

"I don't know!" I sputtered. "Anything! How about crayfish?"

Kailani laughed uncertainly. "*Crayfish.* Oh, Zinny, really—"

"No, I'm serious! Ms. Molina is getting us crayfish in science—"

"You know what, Zinny?" Maisie interrupted. "It's like you have this *idea* we're still best friends. But you don't *act* like one."

"Why? Because I happen to think crayfish are fascinating?"

"No. Because you turn everything into a stupid joke."

"Crayfish are not a stupid joke!"

"Hey." Out of nowhere, Scarlett had stepped into the kitchen. "What's going on?" she asked loudly.

"Nothing," I said, trying to catch my breath. "We're just talking."

"Yeah? Everything okay?" Scarlett put her hands on her hips. With her hair not so short but still raggedy, her eyes seemed extra big and fierce.

Maisie, Kailani, and I nodded.

"Well, I hate to put an end to these festivities, but I'm trying to do homework, so I need some quiet around here. Time to go, guys." Scarlett waved bye-bye at my friends in a definitely snarky way.

Maisie glanced at Kailani, who shrugged. They picked up their backpacks.

"See you, Zinny," Kailani murmured.

"Thanks for helping with the groceries," I said.

"No problem."

Maisie didn't say anything. She didn't even look at me as she walked out the door.

"Nice friends, Zin," Scarlett commented.

Five Years Ago

In second grade, before we've even met Maisie, Kailani gets two baby girl kittens, a gray one and a black one from the same litter. I'm in love with them both. Dad and Aiden are allergic to all animal fur, which means we can't have a dog or a cat. Mom refuses to let me get a lizard, and she says fish don't make decent pets.

So I go over to Kailani's house every afternoon to play with the kittens, who still don't have names. We make up stories about them: how they're orphans with magical powers, how they're princesses under a spell, how they can predict the future if you understand mewing. I like books about real things—starfish and horses—and I play like this only with Kailani. Because we're best friends.

One day Kailani tells me she's naming the kittens Tulip and Daffodil.

"Flower names, to match Zinnia," she says. "And then they'll belong to both of us."

Same Day, Late Afternoon

After Maisie and Kailani left, Scarlett returned to her laptop, and I set up the slow cooker on the kitchen counter. The weird way that conversation with my friends had just gone, all I wanted was to not think, to mindlessly follow a recipe, so I searched online for a chicken dish. With the shopping I'd done, we even had most of the ingredients. I set the dial to high, which meant the slow-cooking would be fast, as if that made any sense. Anyhow, it was the perfect machine for Abnormal Standard Time cooking, I told myself.

In a little while, nice chickeny smells took over the kitchen as Aiden and I started our homework in the dining room. Usually I did math homework first, but that day I just felt like cramming my brain with French vocabulary or something.

J'ai deux meilleurs amies. Mais elles ne sont pas gentilles avec moi. After about ten minutes, I asked my little brother how the cyborg-mosquito project was going, and when it was due. Because it felt like he'd been working on it forever.

He shrugged. "I'm not doing cyborg mosquitoes anymore."

"Why not?"

"Ms. Felsenstein won't let me. She says it has to be how to do a real thing."

Um, like I told you, Aiden. "Okay, so pick something simple, and get it over with! Like How to Tie a Knot. Or How to Make a PB and J. Or what about How to Cook Online Chicken—"

"Those are all boring. Rudy says it should be something cool."

"Yeah? And Rudy is in charge of coolness?"

Aiden shrugged. "So now I'm deciding between How to Use a Grappling Hook and How to Use Suction Cups to Walk on the Ceiling."

I snorted; I couldn't help it. "Aiden, you think those are more realistic than cyborg mosquitoes? Or quicksand?"

"Grappling hooks *are* real. I saw a video on YouTube! And Rudy said he saw one with giant suction cups."

"Yeah?" I didn't know Rudy super well, but he struck me as the sort of kid who made stuff up. And I had the feeling Aiden believed whatever Rudy said. "So what's *his* topic?"

"How to Disguise Yourself to Sneak Past Security."

"*What?* Does Ms. Felsenstein know?"

"He says he didn't tell her yet."

"Yeah, well, Aiden, I have a *very* strong feeling that when he *does*—"

The doorbell rang. My first thought was: Maisie and Kailani. *Sorry we said all that stuff to you an hour ago. Of course we're all friends! And we promise to stop pressuring you, guilting you, stalking you all the time. We'll totally shut up from now on about James Ramos, and we'll stop demanding information about Gabriel! And about the rest of your family too! And yes, please tell us about the crayfish, which sound absolutely fascinating and NOT LIKE A JOKE!*

But by the time I opened the door, no one was there, and a car was driving away.

On the steps were three flats of baby plants, four bulging bags of soil, a small hand rake, and a metal shovel. Each plant had a Popsicle stick poking out of the dirt, on which someone had written in black marker *THYME, ROSEMARY, SAGE, OREGANO, LAVENDER*. And tucked underneath one of the flats was a small white envelope addressed *ZINNIA*.

I opened it.

Dear Zinny,

Tía Marisol picked these for you herself. She insisted on the niece discount, so no charge. ☺

It's early for the growing season, but these herbs are hardy, so they should be okay, I think. Looks like warm weather the next few weeks (boo, climate change ☹) and it's supposed to rain all weekend, so good timing! Have fun!!

Isabella Molina

P.S. LMK if you have any questions! ☺

Inside the envelope was another sheet of paper, neatly folded in thirds: planting directions.

I should probably do the planting right now, I thought. *Before it rains.* French homework could wait.

But how was I supposed to carry all this stuff to the backyard? Especially those bags of soil, which were gigantic.

Then I remembered the little red wagon.

Before Dinner

I am four years old. Gabriel and Scarlett are pulling me up our street in a little red wagon, over and over, in a game they call Prisoner of War. We are yelling and laughing, not caring about the neighbors. And then Mom realizes that I am the prisoner, so she makes them stop. I cry my head off, because I don't care what they call the game, or what they call me; I just want to play with them, be included by my big sister and brother. But now they refuse.

The wagon was rusty now, forgotten in our garage, and one of the wheels was wobbly, but it still worked. In two trips I'd hauled everything to the scraggly garden.

I started pulling up weeds. Some of them were incredibly stubborn. *Assassin vines,* I thought. Well, they weren't going to entrap *me.*

Pretty soon my hands started stinging, so I took a break—and that was when I noticed Mom standing a few feet away, watching me. Her face was pale, and by the way her sweatshirt hung off her shoulders, I could see she'd lost some weight, although maybe that was from all the running. And even in this cloudy light, I could see silver threads in her dark brown hair.

When had her hair begun turning gray? Why didn't she dye it back to normal? It made her seem old, and I didn't like it.

Maybe her therapist will tell her to dye her hair. If she'll even listen.

"Zinny? What's all this?" she asked, smiling.

"I'm clearing out some space for herbs Ms. Molina got from her aunt's nursery. For free." I smiled back at her. "I thought we could use them in some recipes."

"Ms. Molina? That's your science teacher, right?"

I nodded. *Mom never used to forget my teachers' names. Never.*

"Well, what a nice idea," she said. She pushed up the

sleeves of her sweatshirt and squatted next to me. I could see that her gray yoga pants had a Florida-shaped coffee stain. When was the last time she'd washed them? Or any of the other stuff she wore all the time?

Her forehead wrinkled. "Although it's a bit early to be planting. Even around here."

"Yeah, probably," I admitted. "But it's so warm out already, and Ms. Molina checked the forecast. Anyhow, she says these herbs are really strong."

"Well, yes, they are. But don't expect a whole lot of growth. It's not even March yet, sweetheart." Mom pointed. "Can I have that little rake?"

"Sure," I said.

The two of us worked side by side, weeding, raking, poking purple earthworms, and finally planting the baby herbs. I told her about the crayfish, and Tia Marisol's plant nursery, how I needed to visit it sometime to say thank you.

Mom didn't say very much, but she seemed relaxed— more like herself than she'd seemed in weeks, really. Every once in a while she did a few yoga stretches, and a few times I watched her rub her fingers on the tiny lavender.

She caught me watching her, and smiled. "Zinny, did you

know lavender was my favorite scent? Also rosemary. Oh, and basil, too, especially on pizza."

"Maybe when it gets warmer, we can grow some basil! And cherry tomatoes," I said eagerly. "In a pot."

"Or even those big beefsteak tomatoes. Although they take forever."

"Not if we compost! Then we'd have natural fertilizer. Ms. Molina says—"

"She's taught you a lot this year, hasn't she." Mom's eyes had a question I couldn't decipher. "Well, that's wonderful. Good science teachers are so important."

"You're a good teacher too," I blurted. "Your students love you, Mom. When are you going back to work?"

"Soon. Not yet."

"But don't you miss teaching all that Shakespeare? And grading papers? And writing a million college recommendations?" I was teasing Mom, but I could see she didn't mind.

Suddenly she went quiet.

She was staring at the red wagon. Now that all the herbs were in the ground, and the bags of soil used, the wagon was sitting there in the sun, empty.

And it was like my mouth started talking fast. All on

its own, just to fill the silence. "Hey, Mom, remember that game we used to play, Prisoner of War? How Gabriel and Scarlett were pulling me around in that old wagon, up and down the street, until you found out? And then you made them stop, and I threw a giant tantrum—"

Mom closed her eyes.

Oh.

Why had I said that? Reminded her about Gabriel, back when he was okay?

We were having such a nice time together, not thinking about him for a few minutes.

Why did I spoil it?

I patted the soil, like that would change anything.

But a few seconds later, Mom was smiling at me.

"Yes, Zinny, of course I remember," she said.

Sunday Night at Nine Forty-Five P.M.

I tiptoed into Aiden's room and slipped a note into his backpack:

> What to Do If Your Submarine Is on Fire
>
> What to Do If a Very Large Dog Sneezes a Giant
> Wad of Dog Snot in Your Face and You Have No
> Tissue and You're Completely Naked So You
> Can't Even Rub It Off with Your Sleeve
>
> What to Do If the Door Opens When You're in an
> Elevator and a Giant Expanding Marshmallow
> Walks In and Starts Pushing All the Buttons

What to Do If You Get to School and Sit on a Wad of
Gum, Then Realize You Forgot to Wear Pants
What to Do When You're Shipwrecked on a Desert
Island All by Yourself and You Have a Really
Stupid Song Stuck in Your Head

I knew these wouldn't help him pick a topic. But picturing the look on his face when he reached into his backpack tomorrow morning and found this dumb list made me smile.

Monday Morning

Maisie and Kailani never showed up at my front door that Monday, so I walked to school on my own.
And the whole way there I told myself:

> *So what if you aren't friends anymore.*
> *That friendship was nothing but an*
> *   endless fight, anyway.*
> *"We care about your feelings."*
> *No, they don't. Not really.*
> *Because if they did care, they'd care*
> *   about all my feelings,*

Not just the worried ones about
  Gabriel.
They'd want to hear other stuff too,
Other things that are just as real:
Like the dumb names I gave to my
  Barbies,
Why I like science class so much,
Why I'm truthfully so excited about
  getting crayfish.
How nice it was planting herbs with
  Mom,
How good it felt to put that note in
  Aiden's backpack,
Knowing it would make him giggle.
And they'd let me be quiet when I feel
  like being quiet
And just want to be at school, going
  to classes,
Or thinking about herbs
Or crayfish,
Or how maybe all I want is a slice of
  pizza.

Homeroom That Morning

ME: Um, hi.

KAILANI: Hi, Zinny.

MAISIE:

ME: You guys didn't show up this morning.

KAILANI: Yeah, sorry! It was raining, so my mom gave us a ride.

ME: Oh. *(Thinking: It was raining on me, too. And didn't your mom say she wanted to drive me places?)*

MAISIE:

KAILANI: See you later, okay?

ME: Yeah. Okay. See you.

Monday, Lunch Period

"Zinny! Just the person I was waiting for!" Ms. Molina greeted me.

It wasn't the very beginning of lunch period, because this time I'd gone to the cafeteria first so that Ms. Molina wouldn't give me her sandwich again. And I'd gobbled my Swiss-cheese-and-veggie wrap on the way upstairs to the science lab.

Ms. Molina was in her classroom, standing in front of six empty fish tanks.

"They're here?" I squealed. "The crayfish?"

"Tomorrow," she replied, smiling. "They need to travel

carefully. And we need to have everything ready before they get here. Help me with the setup?"

I almost danced.

We spent the next thirty-five minutes assembling the air bubblers and filters. Ms. Molina said the lab was too sunny for the tanks; crayfish liked darker rooms, so while they were with us, we'd keep them in the classroom with the blinds closed. Also, she said, crayfish needed sand to dig in, and places to hide, so we lined the bottom of each tank with sand, then set up a miniature playscape: tipped-over plastic castles, hollowed-out rocks, gerbil pipes, three-sided containers, and fake plants (because they'd eat any real ones).

Gabriel would love this, I thought. *Teeny-tiny Crayfish World!*

So many funny little details. But no little bitty pincer dryers. And no French Revolution bathroom chair.

The bell rang, and kids started walking into the classroom. As soon as they saw the tanks, they got excited.

"Where are they?" Aspen demanded. "I want to meet mine!"

Hers? Wait. There were only seven tanks.

"How many crayfish in a tank?" I asked.

"Just one," Ms. Molina replied. "Crayfish aren't particularly fond of company."

Li-Mei frowned. "What about humans? Does that mean they'll attack us?"

"They'll pinch only if they feel vulnerable. They also do a maneuver called a tail flip, where they escape by flipping their abdomen and swimming backward, pushing mud toward the attacker. So we need to handle them gently and respectfully, avoiding the eyes and tail."

My heart was sinking a little. There were twenty-four kids in the class, and only seven tanks—so that meant four kids to a tank, with the seventh tank for Ms. Molina's crayfish. For some reason, I'd had this vision of my own private crayfish in my own private tank. But that wasn't practical, obviously.

And before I knew it was happening, Ms. Molina was announcing "tank teams."

I was with Aspen, Darius, and (bleh) James Ramos.

Which almost spoiled the whole thing right there.

Until the bell rang, and Ms. Molina came over to my desk. "See you at lunch tomorrow, Zinny?" she asked. "I'll need an assistant to help when the crayfish arrive."

I beamed my answer.

Monday, after School

ME: So? Did you like my note?

AIDEN: Yeah. But those aren't real topics, Zinny.

ME: Of course not! They weren't *supposed* to be, Aidy! They were jokes!

AIDEN: Oh. Well, thank you.

ME: You're welcome! Did you think they were funny?

AIDEN: I guess.

ME: Well, they were! They were *hilarious*, Aiden! And did you think of any others? Something really dumb and silly—

AIDEN *(shakes head)*: I need to think of a real topic, not

jokes. Some kids are finished with their reports already.

ME: *(sighs)*

AIDEN: Okay, but *whyyyy* did that giant marshmallow push all the buttons in the elevator?

Monday Dinner

That evening, Mom made dinner. Nothing fancy, just cheeseburgers, mashed potatoes, and string beans. But it was the first regular family dinner she'd made in weeks, and even Dad was home early enough to join us. And between Dad sitting with us again, and the crayfish, and the way Ms. Molina had invited me to be her assistant—I was so excited I couldn't shut up.

"You know how to tell a male crayfish from a female one?" I asked. I'd spent all afternoon doing online research, so I was gushing with facts.

Scarlett snorted. "The male crayfish explains to the female how to swim?"

Mom smiled. I peeked at Dad; he was smiling too. His real smile this time.

I grinned at my sister. "No, it's that the females have longer leg-thingies. 'Swimmerets.' And speaking of swimming," I continued, "you know what's funny? Crayfish *walk* forward, but they move backward only when swimming."

"Whoa, fascinating," Scarlett said, arranging the lettuce on her cheeseburger. "I'm just, like, totally mesmerized, Zinnia."

"Scarlett," Dad said. Still smiling, though. "No need."

I turned to Aiden. "And want to hear something incredibly cool? Crayfish eyes move independently!"

"I already knew that," Aiden said, chewing.

"You did?"

"Uh-huh. So do mantis-shrimp eyes, but they have better vision. *And* they have blades that can cut the human finger. In *seconds*!"

"Seriously?"

He nodded. "Hey, Zinny, know what else is true? Piranhas can skeletonize an entire cow in under a minute."

"*Okay, enough,*" Mom said in her teacher voice. "Can we please try a more pleasant topic at the table?"

"*Thank* you," Scarlett said.

"Sure." I shrugged. "Although in my opinion, crustaceans are *extremely* pleasant."

"Except when they pinch people," Aiden said.

"Ms. Molina says crayfish won't pinch if they're handled properly. She says they defend themselves by using their pincers. And escape by retreating while pushing mud toward their attackers."

"Nevertheless," Dad said. *"Not supper talk, Zin."*

"Okay." I wasn't even hurt that Dad had spoken sharply to me. It just felt good to have him so . . . there.

No one said anything as we all ate cheeseburgers. I was suddenly super aware that the five of us hadn't eaten together in a long time. It was like we were out of practice, shy with one another, or just awkward. All right, what was there for us to chat about? We needed a conversation starter fast.

And then Mom beat me to it.

"So," she said, "next weekend we're planning another family trip to see Gabriel. Dad and I were thinking of a different motel—"

"I'm not going," Scarlett announced, pushing away her plate.

Mom put down her fork. "Why not?"

"Because I already have plans with my friends. Not everything in my life is about *Gabriel*, you know."

Right away I could tell Scarlett realized how mean that sounded, because her face got red, and she spoke really fast. "Anyhow, I think Gabriel felt weird about the whole family being there last time, like we all drove there just to stare at him. The whole thing was incredibly depressing, and I just want to see him when he's normal."

"We all do, Scarlett," Dad said. He was quiet for a second. "But right now he isn't. And he needs us there."

"To do what? Sit in a creepy room and play Scrabble?"

"Zinny and I played Ping-Pong," Aiden reminded her. I popped my eyes at him like *Not the point, okay?*

"Actually, Scarlett," Mom said, ignoring Aiden, "we were thinking this time you could join us for some family therapy with the social worker."

"Oh, forget *that*," Scarlett exploded. "I'm already doing enough talking with Elyse. Can Gabriel's mental problems please not take up my *entire existence*?"

Mom and Dad traded a long look.

Dad sighed. Then he said, "Okay, but we're not leaving you here alone for the weekend."

"No problem," Scarlett said quickly. "I'll stay over at Jamilla's. Her mom said I could anytime."

Jamilla's mom ran the PTA at Scarlett's high school. And seemed to be in charge of everything else in town too.

Something crossed my mind then.

"You told Jamilla's mom about Gabriel?" I asked Scarlett. "And Redwoods Village?"

"Why not? I'm not ashamed of it, Zinny. Are *you*?" She cocked her head at me and blinked.

"No! Of course not, Scarlett!" I could feel my cheeks burning as I thought about Maisie and Kailani. "But I thought we were all supposed to keep it private—"

"That's right, we are." Mom gave Scarlett a worried look. Then she sighed and patted my hand. "I just think we all need to be careful about who we talk to, and what we say. Not because we're ashamed, which we aren't, but because it isn't anyone's business."

"It's just what's best for Gabriel," Dad added. Although he seemed a little less sure than Mom, I thought.

The other thing I thought was: *So how come Mom added all that stuff when she talked to Rudy's mom—saying Gabriel was "working hard" "back in college?"* Maybe we shouldn't overshare private details, especially with people we didn't trust (like Rudy's mom, for example). But why make up a totally fake story?

That just seemed wrong to me. And unfair to Gabriel.

"I want to see him!" Aiden wailed.

"You will, baby," Mom said. "And so will Zinny." She smiled at me with round, serious eyes.

And I thought how if Scarlett wasn't going, someone would have to stay with Aiden in the indoor recreation center while Mom and Dad did their therapy stuff with Gabriel. So basically I had no choice.

Also, I wondered if Scarlett was right: maybe Gabriel didn't want us all there. But maybe he did.

"Yep, I'm coming too," I told my little brother. "And this time prepare to be *annihilated* at Ping-Pong."

Tuesday

The next morning I didn't bother to wait for Maisie and Kailani. Nothing had happened since yesterday to make me believe they would show up to walk me to school. Besides, the thought of standing on my front step in the windy rain, searching down the block for their umbrellas, was too upsetting.

And it turned out I was right not to expect anything. Because when I got to homeroom, Kailani just gave me a little finger wave. Maisie didn't even look up; she whispered something to Kailani, who shrugged.

So that was that, I told myself. It was obvious my friends

weren't my friends anymore. They were mad because I wasn't acting the way they thought I should—confiding in them, being all weepy in the lunchroom—as if there were one right way to act when your brother went crazy and your family made you keep it a secret. And I was mad at them for being mad at me.

Sometimes the bottom step fell out, and everything changed all of a sudden.

There was nothing you could do when this happened, really.

I used to not know about stuff like this. But now I did.

After an endless morning, the bell finally rang for lunch. Just as I was turning the corner to race upstairs to Ms. Molina's classroom, I almost smacked into Jayden.

"Hey," he said loudly. Then he grinned. "So, will we see you tomorrow?"

Maybe because I was so focused on Ms. Molina and the crayfish, for a second I had no idea what he was talking about.

Also, seeing Jayden's extreme cuteness so close up kind of startled me.

"See me where?" I said.

"You know. Gladys."

"What?" I stared at him.

"Ralph," he explained. "But this week it's Gladys."

"Oh," I said, beginning to realize he was talking about Lunch Club. "I thought it was just Luz who called it that."

"No, I do too. Lunch Club sucks as a name, right? And there isn't really a word for what we do there, so." He shrugged. "Gladys."

Two very tall, very pretty eighth-grade girls called out, "Hi, Jayden!" He waved at them, and they both started giggling.

"Okay?" he said, his dark eyes looking right into mine. "You'll be there, Zinny?"

"I'm not really sure." I wasn't prepared for this decision; plus, eye contact with this boy was making my brain scamper in all directions. "I mean, I kind of promised to help my science teacher—"

"Aw, you can do that anytime. Gladys is just one lunch a week, you know? It's special. And anyhow, Luz needs to reveal the secret handshake."

"I don't know," I said. "Maybe. I'll think about it."

He smiled. "Don't think, Umzinnia. Just show up. Besides, it's really good pizza."

A Few
Minutes Later

Ms. Molina was standing in the middle of the room, her hands on her hips. At her feet were three big coolers, bags of vegetables, and several boxes labeled SHRIMP PELLETS.

She didn't even greet me. "Okay, Zinny," she said, "let's get to work. Since we've already lined the tanks with sand, now we'll add the water and do some testing. The crayfish need a perfectly neutral environment—"

"They're in those coolers?"

"Yes, in plastic bins. But I'm sure they're ready to explore their new digs!"

She showed me how to test the water, make sure all the air bubblers were working, and seal the filters with aluminum foil to keep the crayfish from escaping.

"This is critically important," she said. "Crayfish are explorers. And if they get out of their tanks to wander, they can dehydrate in just a few hours."

I thought about that. You'd think crayfish would know they shouldn't leave their perfect water, that they'd have some sort of survival instinct about that, or something.

Maybe they thought the stay-in-the-fish-tank rule didn't apply to them.

Really, it seemed like such a human mistake to make.

By the start of class, each crayfish was in a separate tank— six for the class, one for Ms. Molina. My team got the tank with the sideways castle, the plastic palm tree, and the hollowed-out rock.

"Omigosh, our crayfish is like a baby lobster," Aspen crooned. "It's so, so cute!"

"It's not a baby anything," I said. "It's fully grown."

"Is it a boy or a girl?"

"Any guesses?" Ms. Molina asked. She carefully lifted our crayfish from the tank.

"It's a male," I blurted. "I looked up crayfish online. Female swimmerets are longer."

Ms. Molina beamed at me.

"What are swimmerets?" Li-Mei asked. She made a face like she didn't believe that was even a real word.

Ms. Molina held up the crayfish. "See those thin, spiny legs below the real legs? In males, they're white-tipped and lie between the last pair of walking legs. Female swimmerets are longer and softer, for holding eggs. So I agree with Zinny—I think you guys have a male."

"Yesss!" Darius pumped his arm, like he was celebrating.

I rolled my eyes. *Scarlett would probably slap this kid,* I thought.

"Can we give them names?" Aspen begged. "Because I already have a good one: Clawed."

"*Excuse* me?" Darius said, laughing.

"That's a pun," Aspen explained. "You know, like the name Claude, only spelled like—"

"Yes, we get it," I cut in. "But I just think if we're doing real science, we shouldn't be naming our subjects. They're not pets."

Ms. Molina put her hand on my shoulder. "Zinnia is thinking like a true scientist. I'll leave the naming question up to you guys: if you feel compelled to name your crayfish, go ahead. But yes, let's keep our relationship with these creatures as scientific as possible."

Aspen wrote *CLAWED* on a strip of masking tape, which she stuck on the tank.

Ugh. How to Survive Working with Aspen Garber.

I tried to focus on Ms. Molina.

"Today," she said, "we'll just be observing, taking notes in our science journals about how they interact with the tank environment. One thing I want you to notice is how sensitive they are to sound. So talk to them."

Darius hooted. "What do we say?"

"Anything at all." Ms. Molina laughed. "You don't need to speak crayfish."

"Do crayfish have ears?" Li-Mei asked.

"No. But that doesn't mean they can't hear."

"What about music?" James Ramos asked.

"Music? You want to play a crayfish *music*?" I didn't even try to hide my scorn. This kid was way beyond stupid.

How to Survive Working with James Ramos.

Ms. Molina didn't seem to notice my face, or my voice. "Interesting question, James. Try singing, and see what happens."

Darius let out a loud, long burp.

Ugh. How to Survive Working with Him, Too.

"Just be sure to record all observations," Ms. Molina said. "Tomorrow we'll be designing some cool experiments. And, Zinny, I'd like to talk to you after class."

Right after Science Class

I was sure Ms. Molina was going to scold me for how I acted with my crayfish team. Instead she waited for everyone to leave the room, and then turned to me, smiling. "You're really into this crayfish study, aren't you," she said.

"Yes," I said quickly. "And sorry if I was rude before. And showing off about the swimmerets. I've just been reading a bunch of stuff online—"

"Never apologize for your passion about a scientific subject. That's not why I wanted to talk to you." Her eyes were sparkling. "Zinny, have you ever heard of Blue Shoals Marine Lab?"

I shook my head.

"Well, every summer they run a four-week program for kids who are really into marine biology. It's not a camp; you do actual research. And it's completely free, because they get a lot of funding. Interested?"

Was she joking? "Yeah. I mean yes, definitely!"

"Awesome," she said. "Because the deadline for applications is approaching, and I wanted to recommend you. You need a letter of support from your science teacher, and that would be me."

Ms. Molina brought over her laptop and showed me a page:

Blue Shoals Summer Program for Middle Schoolers

Spend four weeks with other middle schoolers who share a strong interest in marine biology as you conduct actual research with working scientists. Explore how crustaceans, fish, sea lions, and florae share the ecosystem of our magnificent protected marine lab.

"Just so you know, there's no guarantee you'll get in," Ms. Molina said. "It's extremely competitive. But I'd really love to see you do this, Zinny."

"I'd love to see me do this too," I said.

She grinned. "All right, first I'll need permission from your parents; then I'll get the application going. Of course I'll let you know as soon as I hear anything, but it won't be for a while."

"Okay. Thank you so much!"

"You're very welcome. And, Zinny, try to be a little more patient with your teammates, okay? Group work is so important for scientists."

My cheeks burned. "I know. I'll try."

"Good. Also, I'd prefer if you didn't discuss this Blue Shoals program with classmates. I can nominate only one student, and I don't want to cause any hard feelings."

No problem. I'm really great at keeping secrets.

That Afternoon

As soon as I got home, I looked up more crayfish facts on my computer—stuff about their optimal habitats and behavior. I was thinking maybe I could use some background information to design a good experiment. My teammates wouldn't be doing any research, I knew, so if anyone was going to learn crayfish facts, it was me.

But after about fifteen minutes, Aiden left the table to go to the bathroom, and I found myself typing the words "bipolar disorder."

A lot came up. I mean, way more than I expected. Too much to take in, really.

Bipolar disorder, also called manic-depressive illness, is a brain disorder that causes unusual shifts in mood and energy. Bipolar disorder is not the same as "mood swings," or the normal "ups and downs" associated with adolescence.

People having a manic episode may feel up, jumpy, wired, or agitated; they may talk fast, have trouble sleeping, or engage in risky behavior. . . .

People having a depressive episode may have little energy, feel sad, have trouble sleeping, or sleep too much. . . . Many highly creative, productive people have been associated with bipolar disorder, including Demi Lovato, Carrie Fisher— *Princess Leia?!*—Winston Churchill, Frank Sinatra, Ada Lovelace, Edgar Allan Poe—

Although how did we know that? Did all these people get notes from their doctors?

And did their families make up stories about them, too? *Yes, Edgar Allan is back in college, studying paleontology—*

"What are you reading?" Aiden asked, peering over my shoulder.

"Nothing." I shut my laptop. "Just about crayfish."

"What about them?"

"You know, just how they swim," I said.

A Summer Afternoon, Five and a Half Years Ago

"*A*ll you do is blow bubbles into the water," Scarlett says. "*Like this, see?*"

We are in the four-foot section of the pool. Scarlett's chin is underwater, and she is wearing oversized green goggles, so when she blows bubbles, she looks like a bubbling jellyfish monster or something. I am almost seven years old, and to be honest, even I'm a bit freaked.

"No!" Aiden shouts at her. "I don't see!" He's two and a half, and this is the summer he shouts at everything.

Everyone at the town pool is staring at us. The Manning kids have a reputation for noisiness. And splash fights.

Gabriel does his goofiest grin. "Aww, Aidy, it's okay. Want me to give you a ride on my back?"

"Yes!" Aiden shouts, giggling. He grabs Gabriel's sunburned shoulders.

Scarlett slaps the water angrily. Sometimes she mommies Aiden a little too much, in my opinion. But this time I'm on her side.

"Gabriel, Aiden needs to learn how to swim," I protest. "It isn't safe for him to be in this part of the pool."

Gabriel pushes his wet hair out of his face. "Yeah, and he will learn, Zinny. But he's only two, remember?"

"And a half. He's not a baby!"

Scarlett nods at me. When it comes to this subject, the two of us are a team.

"Aiden can't even tread water yet," she argues. "We should be teaching him, not giving him rides!"

"Well, if you ask me, he needs to have fun," Gabriel insists. "That's how you learn, by liking the water. Otherwise, what's the point of swimming?"

He galumphs through the water with Aiden, the two of them shouting and laughing as they make a tsunami.

Afternoon, Late
This Past August

I knock on Gabriel's door. The music is blaring, so I knock again.

No answer.

"Hey, Gabriel!" I shout. "WANNA GO GET ICE CREAM?"

He doesn't answer.

I pound on the door so hard I hurt my hand.

"HEY, GABRIEL!" I shout, even louder. "I WANT A MONSTER CONE AT HERE'S THE SCOOP. DON'T YOU?"

I hear scuffling; then he opens the door a crack. His eyes look confused, like he's just woken up, even though it's four o'clock, and his room is throbbing with noisy music. And even though his door is barely open, a smell like unwashed socks attacks my nose.

"What is it," he asks flatly. It's not even a question.

"I asked Mom and she says it's okay if we take her car to go get ice cream. I mean, she says if you want to drive—"

He scowls. "Who says I do?"

"Oh. I just thought if you weren't doing anything—"

"Well, I am." His eyes shrink, like they can't bear to take in too much light.

"Like what?" I press him. "What are you doing?"

"Nothing."

"Were you sleeping? I don't know how you could. Because that music is so loud—"

"Zinny, just please go away."

He shuts the door on me.

Wednesday, Lunch Period

I hadn't planned on going to Gladys. In fact, at lunch I went straight to the lab—and the door was locked. I peeked inside the science classroom, but Ms. Molina wasn't there either.

Was she hiding from me? That was a weird thing to think.

Why would she? Especially after telling me about that marine biology program she was nominating me for.

Maybe she was just in the bathroom. Or in the teachers' lounge, eating birthday cake.

I waited five more minutes. I fidgeted with my tiny chair

charm, and smeared on cherry ChapStick. Then I chewed off a hangnail (left pinkie). But she never showed up.

Well, I definitely was *not* going to the lunchroom, that was for sure. Maisie wasn't even making eye contact with me anymore. And every time I passed Kailani, she gave me a sad, helpless little smile. Like, *I'm really sorry, Zinny, I know this is horrible, but what can I do?*

Nothing, I thought. *If you don't want to talk to me anymore, whatever. I don't want to talk to you, either. And definitely not to Maisie!*

So I went to Gladys. At least there I'd get a slice of pizza, I told myself. And see Jayden. Maybe Luz would show me the secret handshake.

And talking about hard stuff—if Gabriel could do it in his therapy sessions, so could I. Maybe.

Anyhow, it was only for thirty-five minutes.

Room 107B was transformed. The sofa and chairs were missing, and the walls were covered in white paper.

"What's going on?" I asked from the doorway.

Luz grinned at me. "Hey, Zin, it's Graffiti Day!"

"What's that?"

Mr. Patrick entered the room behind me.

"Zinny," he said, as if he was stating a fact. He didn't seem surprised to see me. "Why don't you grab a bunch of markers? Today's all about expressing ourselves."

"You mean on that paper?" I waved my arm at the white-covered walls.

"Yep." He smiled. "Pick any free spot, and just express whatever you want, any way you want to. Words or pictures, or a combination. Something abstract, if you'd rather. Or maybe a message to someone—"

"About what?" My heart was speeding. "Do you mean on a specific subject?"

"No rules, okay? Entirely up to you. And nobody has to see your wall if you don't want to share. Today is just about getting it out."

I peeked at the others. Luz had covered nearly the whole wall near Mr. Patrick's desk—a bunch of squiggly hard-to-read words in purple marker. Keira was drawing what looked like a giant rainbow tornado. Jayden was standing over by the window, filling a big green circle with heads speaking dialogue. And Asher was sitting in the corner, writing what looked like a list.

I took some markers from Mr. Patrick's desk and moved over to where Jayden was writing. Not near enough to see what the heads were saying, though; I figured it wasn't my business, unless he wanted to show me.

I uncapped an orange marker.

Orange? Maybe not orange.

Blue.

Blue always cleared my head. Blue helped me think.

I drew some wavy blue lines.

Water.

Wavy blue waves.

A lot of water. A pool, or maybe an ocean.

And bubbles.

Bubbles were kind of fun to draw, actually.

Then a red crayfish waving hi with one pincer. So it couldn't be an ocean. Crayfish swam in running fresh water, in brooks or streams. Or in rice paddies, swamps, or muddy ditches.

Of course, they also swam in tank water.

I drew a giant rectangle around all the blue.

A tank, with all kinds of stuff in it. A pink castle. A green plant. Some rocks in different colors.

Then a crayfish escaping out the top.

A big brown hand grabbing the crayfish.

YOU'RE SAFE NOW, STUPID, I wrote in purple comic book letters.

I stopped.

No one was talking or laughing—the only sound was the *scritch-scritch* of markers. They were all so focused, getting their feelings out into the universe, or at least on this wall—and I was filling up my space with nothing. Waves and bubbles. A comic-book diorama, a total waste of time.

So I ripped it down.

"Sorry, just remembered something," I muttered to Mr. Patrick, and slipped out of room 107B.

Wednesday, Next Period

Ms. Molina was back in the classroom for science. She didn't explain to me where she'd been during lunch, and anyway, it wasn't the sort of question I could ask.

Now she was strolling around, chatting with the tank teams as we debated what our experiments would be.

My team was hopeless.

Aspen wanted to do something about water temperature; what would happen if the water were eighty degrees.

"The crayfish would die," I said. "That's what would happen."

Aspen pouted. "That's just your hypothesis, Zinny. You don't *know*."

She obviously thought that if she used the word "hypothesis," it would make her sound like a scientist.

I didn't want to be rude again, but I didn't want to kill the crayfish, either. "Actually, Aspen, I've read a bunch of stuff," I said carefully. "Crayfish water needs to be between seventy and seventy-five degrees. They're very sensitive to temperature."

Sensitive to temperature, Aspen mouthed.

"Well, what about music?" James Ramos asked.

I groaned inside my head. Was he really going to bring up this question *again*? "What *about* music?"

"You know. If crayfish have a preference."

Darius laughed so hard he almost fell off his chair. "If they have a *preference*? Are you like, serious? *Greatest Crayfish Hits. The Crayfish Top Forty*—"

"Shut up, Darius," James said, blushing. "I just mean, do they like loud songs? Or fast songs? Maybe hip-hop versus classical?"

"But what's the *point* of that?" I couldn't stop myself from asking. "And besides, those are too many variables."

Aspen rolled her eyes. She probably thought my saying

"variables" was like her saying "hypothesis," but it wasn't. Because I wasn't showing off; I meant it. Just thinking about all the different types of music Gabriel listened to—in his room, in the car—made me realize we could never get conclusions that would mean anything. Music preference was such a dumb idea, anyway. It was what you'd come up with if you didn't care about science.

"Okay, Zinny, so what do *you* suggest?" James asked.

"I'm not sure yet," I said. "Probably something about their habitat."

Habitat, Aspen mouthed, rolling her eyes.

"Nah, let's think outside the tank," Darius said, grinning at his dad-ish joke. "Let's see how fast our guy moves on land."

"Hey, cool," James said. His eyes lit up. "We could build a track for him to run on. And give him a goal, something to run toward. Like food—"

"No," I said sharply.

The kids looked at me.

"Okay, what's wrong with it?" Aspen demanded, her hands on her hips.

"Too risky," I said. "Clawed's gills need to stay moist, or he can't breathe oxygen. So he can't be out of the tank for very long. And what if he escapes?"

I nearly pinched myself for using the silly name. But Aspen didn't even seem to notice.

"Zinny, Clawed won't escape if we pay attention," Aspen argued. "If all four of us are right there, watching. We'll be super careful—"

"But that's impossible!" I said. "We can't watch *everything*, even if we want to. Sometimes things just happen!"

"Like what?" Darius said. "What could happen?"

"Anything! What if one of us blinks, or sneezes, or our mind wanders for a second? And then if he gets lost somewhere in the room, he'll dehydrate. And then he'll *die*—"

"How's it going, Team Four?" Ms. Molina was standing by our tank. Her hand pressed my shoulder, as if she was trying to keep me from crashing into the ceiling.

"Not great," Aspen said. "Zinny hates anything we suggest."

"Hmm," Ms. Molina said. She lifted her hand. "Well, what *are* you suggesting?"

Darius and James described their experiment. Weirdly, Ms. Molina seemed to approve. She helped design a track—something with cardboard tunnels—that seemed safe enough, probably. And then we talked about variables—how to measure speed. How long the track should be. Whether we should put a piece of food at the end for motivation. And if so, what sort of food it should be.

By the end of the period, we had a design even I had to admit was kind of cool.

But I still felt weird. Ms. Molina had pretty much ignored my input. Also my feelings.

When the bell rang, she came over to my table. "Zinny, can you stick around for a sec?"

It was one of those non-invitation invitations. I knew I couldn't say no. So I shrugged.

"Everything okay?" she asked in a quiet voice as soon as the classroom was empty.

"I guess," I said.

Ms. Molina met my eyes. "Zinny, the crayfish will be safe, I promise. The experiment will only take a few minutes. I've done this sort of track before, and it's more like a tunnel—"

"Okay," I said quickly. "I mean, I get all that."

"So what's wrong?"

I shrugged again.

"Are you upset because I wasn't around today at lunch?"

I stared at the floor. Her saying it like that made me sound like a sulky baby. I felt my face heat up with shame.

"Not really," I muttered, fingering my miniature chair-charm thingy. "I had something to do then, anyway."

If she knew about Gladys, she wasn't saying. "Well, I'll be in my lab tomorrow. Would you like to join me during lunch, help with the crayfish?"

"Okay, sure!" I couldn't keep the smile out of my voice.

"Good," she said, nodding. "I'll look forward to that, Zinny. But there's a catch."

There was? I chewed my lip.

"If you want to hang out in the lab, you have to go to Lunch Club," Ms. Molina said. "Every Wednesday. And I'll hear from Mr. Patrick if you don't show up, or if you leave early. No Lunch Club, no lab time. Do we have a deal?"

I nodded immediately, because I'd get to be in the lab four days of the week—and anyhow, I knew I had no choice.

Wednesday, after School

"Hey, Zinny," Aiden said excitedly. "You know how I know that thing about piranhas and the cow?"

I looked up from my math homework. "No idea what you're even talking about, Aiden."

He showed me a book he was reading. "I told you before, how they skeletonized the cow! President Teddy Roosevelt saw it happen *with his own eyes*. In the Amazon River. In 1913."

"Huh," I said, refusing to look. "You're not writing about this for your how-to project, are you?"

"Maybe."

"How to Survive an Attack of Piranhas? Aidy—"

He lifted his chin at me. "What's wrong with it?"

Where do I start? It's gross. And not funny!

"What happened to the other ideas you had—the grappling hook and the suction cups?" I asked.

"Ms. Felsenstein said no."

"Did she give you a reason?"

He shrugged. "Everything I want to do she says isn't a real topic. And I think she's getting mad."

"Huh. Did she give you any idea of what she *would* consider a real topic?"

He shook his head. "That's why I'm researching piranhas. Because they *are* a real topic. Teddy Roosevelt was the *president*."

"Okay," I said. "I just think maybe your teacher wants you do something more realistic. And it doesn't have to be about survival, does it?"

"Survival *is* realistic, Zinny."

I caught my breath—just a little, so he couldn't tell.

"Well, sure," I said quickly. "I mean, what about something practical, like How to Keep an Annoying Kid from Staring at You? You could wear a mask on the back of your head with two big scary eyes staring at *him*—"

"That would never work, Zinny."

"How do you know? You could try it on Rudy."

Aiden lifted one shoulder, like my idea wasn't even worth a complete shrug.

"Or you could do it—the staring-mask thing—to keep tigers from sneaking up on you," I said. "It could be like How to Survive If You're Up a Tree and There's a Tiger Beneath You. Or a Bear."

"Why would there be a tiger or a bear?"

"I'm not saying there *would* be. It's probably just Rudy sneaking around, acting annoying, maybe wearing a dumb tiger suit or something. And you don't want him to see you, right? So you set a snare trap—"

"Out of what?"

"I don't know. Dryer lint and banana peels. Gum wrappers. Or marshmallows."

"Zinny, why do you keep talking about marshmallows?"

"Actually, I don't," I said, doing a goofy grin. "I just think they're funny. Don't you, Aidy? All soft and gooey. Even the name 'marshmallow'—"

"Nah, they're not funny at all, really. And that's a dumb topic, anyway." Then his eyes lit up. "Oh, but wait, I know—what about leeches!"

I scrunched up my face. "What *about* leeches?"

"That's the coolest topic, don't you think? How to Escape If You're Attacked by Leeches."

"I don't know, Aiden," I began. "I mean, don't you think Ms. Felsenstein wants you to pick something less . . . disgusting?"

But already he'd started typing. And now he was ignoring me completely.

I studied my little brother. Had he always been this weird—so fascinated with gross things, tales of survival? He'd always liked bathroom jokes, words like "snot" and "barf" and "fart." And he used to think the word "underwear" was the funniest thing ever. Maybe this survival stuff was the next phase, normal third-grade-boy stuff. Weren't they *all* fascinated with this kind of thing—lightning and caves, people-eating plants, quicksand, hailstorms, earthquakes? Things that were real, but not so realistic?

Sure, I told myself.

Or maybe this was something else.

That Night

When Scarlett and I were both in our beds, in the dark, I asked her a question: "When was the last time you felt really happy?"

She thought about it for a few seconds.

"I don't know," she finally said. "Definitely before Gabriel."

She didn't need to explain; I knew "Definitely before Gabriel" was a complete sentence.

"Maybe last summer, when we went to the beach," she added. "Why?"

I told her I was worried about Aiden, his obsession

with survival stories, how he was dragging out his dumb assignment. And then I talked about the rest of us: Dad, who'd gone so silent and invisible. Mom, who still wasn't back at work.

I didn't say: *You, Scarlett, who's always so moody.* Or *Me, who's lost my best friends.* But I think she got the drift.

"I wonder if we've all changed because of Gabriel," I said. "Like our brains are different now, maybe."

"I don't know," Scarlett said. "But I guess it would be weird to go through this and *not* change."

"I guess."

We were quiet for a while.

Then I said, "Gabriel changed, didn't he? It started last summer, I thought."

"Well, in a way," Scarlett said slowly. "He was definitely depressed at the end of August. But I think maybe this bipolar thing started before that."

This surprised me. Scarlett had acted like "this bipolar thing" was just some excuse Gabriel made up for getting into trouble. But now that I thought about it, she hadn't said stuff like that in a while. Not since she'd started seeing that therapist of hers. Elyse.

"But last summer," I said. "He was okay sometimes too,

wasn't he? Remember how he joked during the Annual Kid Photo—"

"I guess," Scarlett said carefully. "But what I really think is, he was hiding a lot."

"Hiding?"

"Well, sure, Zinny. You know how he was. Not big on communication. And doing stupid stuff out of nowhere, then feeling sorry about it afterward. Like that time with Mom's car and the gas tank."

"Yeah, that was really bad. Dad got so mad at him." I chewed my lip. "Scarlett, can I ask you a question? Do you think Mom and Dad should have noticed more? Before he got worse?"

It was a question I hadn't even known I was wondering about until I heard my own voice. Maybe I wouldn't have asked this if the lights had been on and I could see my sister's face.

Scarlett took a few seconds before she answered. "You're asking if I'm mad at them?"

"I don't know, I guess," I said.

"I don't know either. Sometimes I am, probably. Because they're his parents, you know? But it's not like *I* got it either. I mean, I saw some things, but I didn't understand what they *meant*."

"Yeah, me too. One time when we went out for ice cream—"

"Let's not talk about this anymore," Scarlett interrupted.

"Oh," I said. "Okay."

We were both quiet.

Then Scarlett said, "Because the truth is, I just get upset at myself."

"For what?

"Not getting it. Not saving him. I don't know."

"Scarlett, you just said Gabriel hid his feelings from us, right? And also did stuff out of nowhere. So how *could* you have—"

"I know, I know! But sometimes I wonder. And then I feel guilty." In the dark I saw her grab a tissue from a box next to her bed and wipe her nose. "You want to hear something else I can't stop thinking? Gabriel was supposed to teach me how to drive. He *promised* me."

"Yeah, well, maybe he's not the world's best driving teacher."

We both laughed. As horrible as it was to joke about something like this, it also felt good, in a strange way.

"Did I tell you I'm doing driver's ed at school now?" Scarlett asked.

"No, you didn't. That's great, Scar."

"I guess. I really want my license, so I'm not waiting for Gabriel to get out of that place."

We got quiet again. And suddenly I heard myself saying: "You know, you really should visit Gabriel when we go this weekend."

"Maybe." My sister sighed. "But to be honest, it sort of freaked me out. Anyway, we text each other constantly, like fifty times a day."

"You mean you and Gabriel? I thought they took away his phone."

"Yeah, when he first got there. But now they let him have it again."

"They *did?*"

"Uh-huh. We never talk about anything important, though. Just stupid stuff to make him laugh."

That made me feel better. A little. I mean, I was glad Gabriel had his phone again. But it also hurt that I hadn't known about it.

And it sort of reminded me of the red wagon—Gabriel and Scarlett excluding me from their fun. Pushing me away at the last minute, making me feel like a little kid.

A few minutes later Scarlett was snoring. But I couldn't

sleep. My brain was flashing back to August—the four of us kids lined up on the stairs for Dad's photo, leaning into one another, when suddenly Gabriel did his Early Manning thing.

Slumping over was a stupid joke—but maybe we laughed mostly out of surprise.

Sometime Last October

Gabriel is in his room, home from college for the weekend. His door is closed. Music is blaring. Mom and Dad yell at him to turn it down. He keeps it loud.

He's sleeping past noon. And now I hear Mom and Dad in his room, shouting at him.

"What's going on with you?" Dad is asking. "Are you even going to classes?"

Gabriel answers, but I can't hear it.

"Are you trying?" Mom asks.

"Why can't you give us a good answer?" Dad asks.

Can't hear.

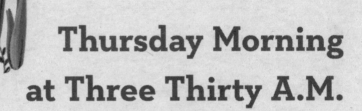

Thursday Morning
at Three Thirty A.M.

I couldn't sleep, so I made another list for Aiden's backpack. Anything to get him off this leeches thing, and to finish the dumb assignment.

And maybe not be so silly this time, because silly wasn't working for him.

So I made it survival-y, but not too leeches-and-quicksand. A bit more realistic.

How to Make a Lean-to for Shelter

How to Make a Bow and Arrow out of Sticks and
    Twine

How to Purify Water Using Evaporation (You need a
paper cup and Saran Wrap)
How to Navigate Using the Stars
How to Ward Off Bears (They stand up when they're
mad! Run away!)

Thursday Morning, Outside Homeroom

"Zinny, can I please talk to you?" Kailani was waiting outside our homeroom. She looked extra pretty that day in her red sweater, and her eyes were big and soft, almost pleading.

I looked around quickly: no Maisie. "Sure," I said. "What's up?"

"I'm just wondering what's going on," she blurted.

"With what?"

"With *us*. We never see you anymore. You're never at lunch—"

"Whoa, wait a second, Kailani! *You* stopped talking to

me. You and *Maisie.* Don't you remember? You accused me of not telling the truth, or talking about stupid, irrelevant things all the time—"

"I never used the word 'stupid.'"

"Okay, but Maisie did."

"Well, we were both just really frustrated with the way you kept pushing us away, so maybe we said some things!" Kailani's voice wobbled and her eyes got teary. "We didn't mean to hurt you, Zinny, and if we did, I'm really sorry. Because I never thought it would turn into *this*—"

"What's 'this'?" I asked bitterly. "'This' isn't anything."

"That's what I'm saying! We're supposed to be friends, and we aren't even talking anymore!" Now she was flat-out crying, and Darius was walking toward us.

My throat was getting tight. "Yeah? Well, why is *that*, Kailani? *I* never stopped talking to *you*. And by the way, in case you forgot, you guys stopped walking with me to school."

"Because we didn't think you wanted to walk with us anymore!" She wiped her face with the back of her hand. "Zinny, can I ask you something? Do you *want* to be friends again?"

"I guess," I admitted. "But what about Maisie? Does she?"

"Yes, but you know how she is." Kailani gave a shaky sigh. "And she has a really hard time apologizing, so."

I stared. "I'm not sure what you're saying."

"I don't know, Zinny . . . How about if you say something to Maisie? Be the bigger person? I mean, who cares who apologizes first? If it makes us all friends again—"

"Wait. *Wait.* Are you saying *I* should apologize to *Maisie*?"

"It's not a big deal! You kind of *did* act like you thought we were dumb for liking James Ramos. And you even said that you thought he was stupid—"

"Because he *is*. Do you know he wants to do an experiment on *crayfish music taste*?"

Li-Mei and Aspen walked past us into homeroom. You could tell they were being quiet so they could eavesdrop better.

"Whatever," Kailani said, lowering her voice to an almost whisper. "The point is, I just want us all to get past this fight, or whatever it is. And if the only thing that's stopping it is a little apology . . ."

"From *me*?"

My brain was whirling. I couldn't apologize. I couldn't say the thing that would make them happy, because it would make me *un*happy.

"Sorry," I told Kailani. "That's just not . . ."

I searched for a word.

"Realistic," I said.

In the Stairwell, on the Way to Lunch

"Umzinnia!" someone shouted. So of course right away I knew who it was.

Even so, the shock of it made my insides freeze. And then someone banged into my backpack.

I caught my balance, and my breath. "Hey, Jayden," I said. "What's up?"

He smiled. "I was going to invite you to my Bad Movie party, but you ran out of Gladys before I could talk to you. Luz is coming, and maybe Keira, and some other kids. It's tomorrow night at my house."

"What's a Bad Movie party?"

"What it sounds like. We watch bad movies and throw popcorn."

"Um, sure," I said. *Idiot. He must think you begin every sentence with "um."* "Should I bring anything? Popcorn? Bad movies?"

"No, we're all set." He wrote something on a scrap of paper he pulled out of his pocket. "My address. See you tomorrow?"

"Yeah. Tomorrow. Thanks."

I ran up the stairs, grinning.

Thursday, Lunch

"Zinny, come quick! You have to see this!"

Ms. Molina was standing over the tank with the extra crayfish. Even though I'd tried to argue, all the other crayfish in our class had names—ours was Clawed, and there was also Cray-Z, Crayola, Ray, Sugarlumps (don't ask), and Ashleigh (ditto). The extra crayfish was Ms. Molina's, so she didn't give it a name—or, if she did, she kept it to herself.

I peered through the glass. The Unnamed Crayfish seemed to be just lying on the bottom of the tank, with its tail curled up.

"I think he's getting ready to molt," Ms. Molina was saying excitedly.

"How can you tell?"

"Just a feeling. He stopped eating, he's hiding under the plants, and if you look closely, his legs look like they're fanning in place."

"So this means he's shedding his exoskeleton? Can I touch it?"

"No," Ms. Molina answered firmly. "It's a very sensitive process. Crayfish feel extra vulnerable while they're molting, and also just afterward, when their shells are still soft. We can observe, but we shouldn't touch. Here." She pushed a notebook toward me. "This is what you can do: take notes."

But about what? Not much was happening. No matter how hard you stared.

The crayfish seems uncomfortable, I wrote. *Unhappy, although that's probably the wrong word. Crayfish are sensitive, but not emotional. I'm sure he doesn't understand what's happening to him. Or why.*

Because he can't think: "Oh, right: last time I felt like this, I got a cool new shell. So I know it's going to be okay."

He just has to go through it.

Lying there on the sand, moving his swimmerets.

Waiting to change.

Still waiting.

Still waiting.

"Why do they molt?" I blurted.

Ms. Molina was typing on her laptop, but she stopped to turn to me. "Because they've outgrown their exoskeleton. It's just part of their life cycle."

"Is it painful?"

"I wouldn't know," she said, smiling a little. "I guess when anything's happening to *you*, it can be."

"And do some crayfish not make it?"

"You mean during molting?"

I nodded.

"I think that can happen sometimes, but it's unusual. Most healthy crayfish molt with no problems, unless they're eaten by a predator. But I suppose if a crayfish isn't feeling well, the process of molting can be extra stressful." She paused. "Why are you asking, Zinny?"

"I don't know," I said.

Thursday and Friday Science Class

So we ran the experiment on Clawed. On Thursday we did all the planning—setting up the track, figuring out how to measure speed, and deciding how to motivate him to the finish line. Darius was the one who suggested we dangle a bit of hot dog on a string—I voted against it, arguing that hot dogs were horrible, full of chemicals probably dangerous to crayfish. (I didn't know this for a fact, but it made sense to me.) Anyway, I said, crayfish preferred shrimp pellets, vegetables, algae, and small fish they could capture with their claws.

But Aspen said crayfish were omnivores—you could tell

how proud she was to know that word—and had a strong sense of smell, so we needed something really smelly to get Clawed moving. James Ramos said he personally loved hot dogs (as if that were the slightest bit relevant), and we were using just a tiny chunk of hot dog, so how much harm could it do? Finally I gave up, because it was obvious by then that no one in the group was listening to me anyway.

On Friday we let Clawed out of his tank.

I held my breath as he moved slowly, zigzagging his way through the covered cardboard track—until he made it to the end.

We ran the experiment five times, so we could get Clawed's average speed.

And, incredibly, all five times he ate the disgusting hot dog.

Saturday Morning at Redwoods Village

Gabriel had scrambled eggs at breakfast, I had a corn muffin, and Aiden had pancakes again. Mom and Dad both had toast and coffee.

We discussed the following topics:

Gabriel needing new jeans and socks.

The too-warm-for-March weather.

Some true-crime podcast Mom was listening to on her runs.

How my science teacher had nominated me for a special summer program.

A basketball team (not the Warriors) that was doing better than anyone had expected.

Gabriel's high school friend Jack, whose mom said he was planning to visit Gabriel sometime soon, although she didn't say when.

We did not discuss:

The fact that Jack knew about Gabriel's secret.

Scarlett not being there.

The teen girl at the next table throwing a tantrum (raisins in her oatmeal).

Whether Gabriel was feeling better.

When he would be getting out.

After breakfast, the five of us took a walk over to see the rock wall and the ropes course. Then Mom, Dad, and Gabriel went to their therapy session.

Wins at Ping-Pong:

Me: eleven games

Aiden: seven

Afterward, Gabriel walked us to the car. "I'm glad you came, Monkeygirl," he told me as we hugged good-bye.

"So am I," I said, because that's what you were supposed to say.

"Tell Scarlett hi."

"Yeah, I will. She'll probably come next time—"

"Maybe better if she doesn't," Gabriel said. "She's really sensitive."

And I'm not?

Of all the things Gabriel had ever said to me, that was maybe the most surprising. I knew he didn't mean it in a bad way, but I still felt crushed.

Did he think I thought visiting him was easy? I had nothing to do at Redwoods Village but babysit Aiden. And seeing Gabriel so pale and un-Gabriel-like made my heart hurt. Did he still think of me as the toddler in the red wagon, the little kid on the sofa afraid of spooky attics? Did he think I didn't get why he was here—basically trapped in a tank and not allowed to leave?

Or that I had nothing going on with *me*?

And it was right then, that very second in the parking lot, that I realized I'd completely forgotten about Jayden's Bad Movie party.

Saturday, Five Thirty P.M.

The second I dragged myself into the bedroom, Scarlett asked how it went.

"Okay," I said.

"Did Gabriel mention me?"

"Yep."

She closed her laptop. "Well, so what did he say?"

"He said hi." At that moment I was too upset with everyone, but especially with my big brother and my big sister, to repeat the whole thing about how Scarlett didn't have to go to Redwoods Village because she was too "sensitive."

Scarlett's face scrunched. "And how was Mom?"

"Mom?"

"Yeah. Did she cry? You know I totally lose it when she does."

"Scarlett," I said, my voice rising, "if you care so much about all the details, next time you should visit Gabriel yourself."

That shut her up for the rest of the evening.

Monday Morning, before Homeroom

ME: Um, hi. Sorry I missed your party on Friday. Something . . . came up.

JAYDEN *(frowning)*: No problem. Everything okay?

ME: Oh, definitely. Everything's great. Well, see ya!

JAYDEN: Wait, I brought you something.

ME: You did?

JAYDEN *(handing me a sandwich bag full of popcorn)*: I didn't know if you liked butter or salt, so I left it plain.

ME *(grinning so much it's hard to talk)*: Plain is fine! Thank you so much!

JAYDEN: You're welcome. See you Wednesday?

ME *(stuffing popcorn into mouth)*: Mnnn, scrmpfth.

That Wednesday, Lunch Period

"You know what, folks? The weather's too great to be stuck indoors," Mr. Patrick was saying. "What say we do Lunch Club *al fresco*."

"You mean like spaghetti?" Jayden asked.

Luz swatted him. "No, you dope, that's *al dente*. 'Al fresco' means 'in the fresh air.'"

"I thought Al Fresco was some guy," Keira said.

Luz grinned. "Yeah, right. Albert Fresco. That's what we'll call it next week."

"No, *Alfredo*."

"Alfredo is the name of a pasta sauce," Jayden said.

"It is, but I think it was named after some dude who

invented it, Alfredo." Keira did a Disney princess sigh. "You know what my dream is? A pasta sauce named after *me*."

"Waiter, I'll have some Elbows Keira," Jayden said.

"*Al dente*," Luz added, laughing. "And we'll eat it *al fresco*."

As we walked out of the building, I glanced at Asher. In the group, we were the only ones not joking around, keeping quiet. I was still feeling mad at myself about forgetting Jayden's party, mad at Mom and Dad for making me spend all Saturday at Redwoods Village, when Scarlett got to stay at her friend's house. And Asher was . . . just being Asher, I guessed.

Mr. Patrick led us to a small clearing behind the soccer field. When Luz plopped down on the grass, he said, "Nah, no loafing, folks. Today's session starts with getting our hearts pumping."

"My heart pumps fine already," Luz protested.

"Okay, but let's get it *really* going. Up to you how— running, dancing, jumping jacks, however you feel like moving. Come on, you guys, three minutes, no stopping."

Mr. Patrick began doing jumping jacks. Luz and Keira did a sort of hip-hop dance. Asher jogged in place (not very enthusiastically), while Jayden and I ran four times around the building. He was faster than me, so it wasn't like we were running together, but once, he turned around and smiled.

"Try to catch up, Umzinnia," he said. And I smiled back, wondering if it meant anything that he'd saved me some popcorn.

After three minutes, Mr. Patrick waved his arms over his head. "All right, folks, gather round. Now that we're energized, I thought we'd play a game." He reached into his pants pocket and took out one of those squishy stress balls they sometimes hand out for free at pharmacies.

"It's called Mad-Sad-Glad," he said. "And the rules are simple. I toss the ball to someone, and whoever catches it names one thing they're mad, sad, or glad about. The idea is *no thinking*: it should be the first thing that pops into your head. Then you immediately toss it to someone else. Pretend this ball is on fire, so you want to get rid of it right away. This game is played very fast."

"It sounds stupid," Luz said.

"Oh, it is. Dumbest game ever." Mr. Patrick flipped the small red ball to Luz. "Go."

"Me?"

"Hurry, Luz, this thing is on fire, remember?"

"Fine. I'm mad that we're playing this stupid game." She tossed the ball to Jayden.

JAYDEN: I'm glad that the weather's nice, even though it's climate-change-nice.

KEIRA: I'm glad we're outdoors for once.

MR. PATRICK: I'm mad because my husband got another parking ticket.

ASHER: I'm mad because I failed a math test.

LUZ: You did? I thought you were this super math nerd.

MR. PATRICK: Stay inside the game, Luz.

LUZ: Sorry. I'm sad I messed up the game just now. Not really.

ME: I'm glad about the crayfish experiments in science. Even though I don't like my team.

KEIRA: Why?

ME: Because they don't listen. And they gave our crayfish a dumb name.

JAYDEN: I'm sad that my dad is back in the hospital.

LUZ: Oh no. Well, I'm sad that you're sad, Jayden.

JAYDEN: Thanks. I'm really glad you're my friend.

LUZ: *Awww.*

KEIRA: Hey, Jayden. Hello? Remember *me*?

JAYDEN: You thought I forgot you?

KEIRA: Well, you and Luz are acting like—

MR. PATRICK: Stay in the game, folks.

JAYDEN: Right. I'm mad you thought I left you out, Keira. I didn't. I was just answering Luz—

KEIRA. Nah, I'm only teasing. I'm glad we're friends too. And sad about your dad.

ME: Me? I just went.

KEIRA: Your turn anyway. Go.

ME: Um . . . I'm still mad that my friends want me to apologize when I didn't do anything wrong.

LUZ: So why should you apologize?

ME: Exactly.

LUZ: Yeah, exactly.

ASHER: I'm mad I'm here. I hate this group.

MR. PATRICK: I'm sad you feel that way, Asher.

ASHER: Well, I do. I'm mad we're wasting so much time.

LUZ: All right, so what would you rather be doing?

ASHER: I don't know. Something that actually helps.

LUZ: Throw the ball to me.

LUZ: Hey, Asher. I'm sad your stepdad is so mean to you. But you should be mad at *him*, not at us, you know?

ASHER: I'm not mad at you.

LUZ: Yes, you are. Every week you come here and grump at us. Like it's our fault.

MR. PATRICK: Rules of the game, Luz.

LUZ: Fine. Asher, I'm sad you're mad at us, because we're here to listen to you. We're the ones who *can*, you know?

ASHER: *(grunting sound)*

KEIRA: I'm glad Luz said that, because I totally agree. Asher, you shouldn't take it out on us. Also I'm mad at my parents, for having such a crappy divorce and making my sister Jocelyn and me have to deal with it all the time.

JAYDEN: *All* the time? You mean like a hundred percent of every minute?

KEIRA: Okay, eighty-four percent. Eighty-seven percent.

JAYDEN: You used to say ninety-eight percent.

KEIRA: Yeah? Well, progress, I guess.

ME: Again? Well, I'm not mad at anyone else. Just my friends. Former friends.

KEIRA: Not your brother?

ME: What?

KEIRA: You know. For what he did to your family.

ME:

KEIRA: When he went nuts and smashed up that car. *On purpose.*

LUZ: *Omigod.* Keira! I can't believe you just said that!

MR. PATRICK: All right, folks—

KEIRA: I'm just saying if my big sister did that to *me*, I'd never forgive her. Ever.

LUZ: Yeah, well, that's *your* feelings, not Zin's! And totally *not* how to bring it up here!

KEIRA: Don't yell at me, Luz!

LUZ: Well, you shouldn't have said that, Keira!

KEIRA *(red-faced)*: Sorry, okay? God. What do you want me to—

MR. PATRICK: Keira, try to calm down. Luz, let it go. Zinny, is there anything *you* want to say here?

ME: Me? *No!*

MR. PATRICK: Okay. It's completely your choice.

ME: Well, I *don't* want to discuss it!

MR. PATRICK: That's fine.

ME: Because Keira doesn't know how I feel, okay? *Nobody* does.

LUZ: So how *do* you feel?

ME: What?

JAYDEN: Don't force her, Luz.

LUZ: I'm not forcing anybody! I'm just asking if she wants to tell us.

ME: I *just* said *I don't want to discuss it*! Why is that *so* hard for everyone to understand?

ME *(catching my breath)*:

ME: And how do you guys know about my brother anyway?

KEIRA: Everyone knows. People talk about things.

ME:

ME: Well, he didn't smash the car *on purpose*! Gabriel wouldn't try to hurt himself! *Okay?*

LUZ: Okay, Zin.

ME: And people don't know *everything*, even if they think they do!

ME:

ME:

MR. PATRICK: All right, well, folks. I see the period is almost over, and we've kind of exhausted the format here. Why don't we all stop by the office for a quick slice of pizza—

LUZ: You mean it's over? Hallelujah.

ASHER: I hated it. And so did Zinny. Let's not do it again.

MR. PATRICK: Deal. Okay with you, Zinny?

ME:

Afterward

Of course I didn't "stop by the office" for pizza. I couldn't eat anything. Or do much of anything all afternoon, even in science.

Keira's questions had punched me in the chest. Had Gabriel done what she said—*smashed the car on purpose*?

Like . . . to hurt himself?

I didn't know. It hadn't even crossed my mind before she said it. So whoever had told her that was making it up, or else knew something I didn't. But who would that be? Nobody. Because he was *my brother*.

And her other question was almost as shocking: Was I

mad at Gabriel? To be honest, I hadn't known being mad at him was even an option.

One thing I knew for sure, though: going back to Lunch Club again was absolutely not possible. Because what right did those kids have—people who weren't my friends, who I'd never even spoken to before in my entire life—to tell me how I should be feeling? Or even to force me to describe it?

What exactly was I supposed to say? Mad-Sad-Glad didn't tell you anything. There wasn't a scientific name for my emotions, some long chewy Latin-sounding word that got more and more specific as it zoomed in on my heart. *Sadnessalia numbveria confusoria worryatum.*

And my feelings kept changing, anyway. Sometimes I didn't feel anything at all. Sometimes I was even happy, like when I was helping Ms. Molina in the lab. So, was that happiness—even if it lasted just an eye blink—supposed to go into the scientific name too? Or would people be all, *How dare you distract yourself, Zinny? You should be a sobbing mess every single second!*

My best friends—scratch that: former best friends—couldn't understand this. So why would almost-total strangers?

Because, yeah, I knew they were all in Lunch Club for a reason. But it wasn't *my* reason.

When I got home that afternoon, I did a strange thing. I went over to the stairs where Dad had hung the Annual Kid Photos: the Four Stages of Manning. These photos—eight of them, all framed—I had to pass every day, on my way up and down, back and forth, to my bedroom. But ever since Gabriel's accident, I'd stopped seeing these pictures. It was like a choice my eyes had made: *Just look forward. Don't focus on anything but what's right in front of you.* And only now that I was back home after that horrible Lunch Club game could I actually look sideways, at what was on the wall.

The photos of all of us, but especially Gabriel.

His deep-set hazel eyes.

His slightly crooked nose (a basketball accident).

His hair: too long, or way too short (he cried that time after the barbershop).

His Christmas-tree smile. Even in that end-of-August photo, when according to Scarlett, he was depressed.

Gabriel was always the kid in the foreground, the one we leaned on. Not a perfect person, but a very good brother.

But still, it was like one day Gabriel just went blank on us. How could he do that? Scarlett said he'd never been "big on communication," but that wasn't an excuse, really. You needed to *tell* your family if things were going that bad for you. Because they needed you to be okay. *We* needed *Gabriel* to be okay. Every single one of us: Mom, Dad, Scarlett, Aiden, and me. And shutting the door on us, smashing the car, was just cruel. Also selfish.

It shocked me to realize I was thinking this: *Maybe Keira was right. Maybe I should be mad at Gabriel.*

But I knew that even if it was true, even if I was mad at my big brother, it was only in one miniature room of my heart.

Wednesday, Late Afternoon

After about an hour of homework (all right, more like twenty minutes) I was starting to feel light-headed from not eating all day, so I made myself a giant, blobby peanut-butter-and-banana sandwich. The bread was sort of stale, but adding peanut butter was such a good distraction that I didn't even mind that the banana was mushy. And while I was chewing, I started a shopping list for Mom: *Bread. Peanut butter. Bananas. Stuff for dinner.*

Because, without even looking in the refrigerator, I knew that once again there was nothing planned for our meal. After Mom had cooked that cheeseburger dinner, it was like she'd said to herself, *Okay, well, I've done that cooking business again—on to the next thing.* And as far as I could tell, the "next thing" on her to-do list was more running, followed by listening to more true-crime podcasts on the sofa.

I mean, I knew Mom was doing better these days. She'd begun taking care of laundry and emptying the dishwasher again. But the only time she left the house was to go for a run, or to pick up a few things at the grocery: yogurt, milk, eggs, bread, spaghetti, Cheerios, more microwave dinners—enough food so we wouldn't starve, but not the kind of cooking she used to do for the family. Also, there was no sign she was getting ready to go back to work. She never mentioned her teacher friends, or talked about her students or any of the Shakespeare plays they'd been studying.

Dad was pretty much the same as Mom lately—definitely better, more like himself, but not all the way back to normal. He ate dinner at home with us half the time now; when he was at the table, I could tell he was trying hard to chat with us about school. But sometimes when I looked in his eyes, I could tell his mind was wandering. And the place it was wandering to was Redwoods Village.

So yeah—it felt weird to think this way about my parents. But it hurt my feelings that they were still tuning everything out. Pushing us away. Except for Gabriel, of course.

And that day, Aiden was really upset and needed to talk to someone. By now, he admitted, the kids in his class were almost finished with their how-tos, which they'd been sharing over the past three weeks. And the thing was, Aiden still didn't even have a topic. Ms. Felsenstein said he needed to stay inside during recess to work on it with her, but when he started crying, I guess she felt sorry for him (*Did she know about Gabriel?*) and let him go. Afterward, though, she told him next Friday was the Absolute Final Deadline: if Aiden didn't do his demonstration in front of the class by then, no recess for two whole weeks.

"Wait," I said. "You need to do a whole *demonstration*? You mean *show* how to do the thing?"

Aiden nodded. His eyes were huge. "Yeah, Zinny. That's how we share it with the whole class."

"Aiden, you never told me that part." I could see how shaky he was, so I tried to keep my voice calm. But inside I was shouting at him: *Why didn't you tell me you needed to demonstrate the how-to? If I'd known that, I wouldn't have let you consider cyborg mosquitoes, and leeches, and all that other stuff. And I wouldn't have spent so much time joking about marshmallows!*

So there I was in the kitchen, suggesting no-joke topics to Aiden (all of which he thought were boring and uncool) while at the same time scribbling dinner items Mom would be buying if she weren't podcasting away the afternoon, when the doorbell rang.

"I'll get it!" Aiden yelled before Scarlett could yell at him to stop yelling.

I heard my little brother say "Really?" and "Whoa."

Then he returned to the dining room grinning, carrying an extra-large-size pizza box from Thom's Pizza.

"You guys ordered?" Scarlett asked, walking into the dining room.

I shook my head.

"There's a note on the box," Aiden announced. "It says 'To Zinny'—"

"It does? Let me see." I snatched the note taped to the box.

> To Zinny,
>   Because you missed lunch.
> See you next week,
> Alfredo

"Who's Alfredo?" Scarlett demanded, reading over my shoulder.

"No one," I said quickly.

"There's a boy at school named Alfredo?" Aiden asked.

"No, Aidy, there isn't."

"So who sent it, then?" Aiden opened the box and helped himself to a slice.

"Ms. Molina," I blurted. "It's from her pet tarantula. A Rio Grande gold. From Texas."

Scarlett burst into a laugh. "Zinny, your teacher has a *pet tarantula* named *Alfredo*? Are you *serious*?"

"Why is a tarantula sending us pizza?" Mom had gotten off the sofa and was now standing in the dining room, looking confused.

"It's really just from Ms. Molina," I said helplessly. "Remember how she gave us all those plants?"

"How come she keeps giving you so much stuff?" Scarlett asked. "My teachers never give *me* anything but homework."

"I bet she thinks Zinny's a genius," Aiden said.

Scarlett lifted an Eyebrow of Doubt.

"Well, we definitely need to thank her," Mom said.

"No, she doesn't want that," I said desperately. "She told

me! She was very clear! Mom, don't you want a slice?"

Mom glanced at the pie. "Maybe later," she said. "I'm not so hungry right now."

"Come on, Mom, you need to eat," Scarlett said.

"I know, honey. I will. Later."

But she didn't sound very convincing. And the way Scarlett caught my eye, I could tell she wasn't convinced either.

Then I thought of something. "Hey, Mom, remember how we said we'd plant some basil when it gets warmer? To put on pizza?"

"I remember," Mom said. "I'm really looking forward to that, sweetheart."

"Okay, but for now, how about some *other* fresh herbs? We have thyme and rosemary, right?"

Mom smiled. "I do love rosemary."

"Yeah, but on pizza?" Scarlett made a face.

I ignored it. I ran outside to the garden. The herbs hadn't grown much since we planted them—not at all, really. But they hadn't died, either. And they smelled delicious, like rain and earth and not-far-off spring.

I pinched off a few sprigs of rosemary and ran into the kitchen. Did you need to rinse off herbs if there wasn't any insecticide on them? Better to be safe, I thought, so I washed the tiny sprigs, quickly dried them in a paper towel, tore them up into tiny pieces, and then went back into the dining room with a fistful of herb bits.

"Madame, for you," I said as I opened my hand over the pizza.

Green confetti rained down over mozzarella and tomato sauce.

Mom gasped. "Oh, Zinny! How wonderful!"

As we watched Mom eat the pizza, Scarlett sneaked me a small under-the-table thumbs-up.

Wednesday Night

That night when we were in bed, Scarlett asked me again about Alfredo. But I still didn't tell her.

"Fine, be that way," she said. Not sounding mean or angry, just sort of disappointed that I wasn't telling her stuff. Which made me feel un-sister-ish.

The truth was, I was sure the pizza was from Luz and Jayden, because the whole thing about renaming Lunch Club was their joke. Also, I could tell they'd both felt bad about Keira's question, and they'd obviously noticed that I'd never shown up in room 107B for a slice.

But I didn't want to talk to Scarlett about Lunch Club. For two reasons.

One: After today I was set on quitting—even if it meant breaking the deal with Ms. Molina and therefore not hanging out in her lab.

Two: I wasn't sure I could mention Jayden without Scarlett noticing my feelings. My sister's crush radar was always turned up to High—and if she ever did find out I liked him, she'd never stop teasing me about it.

Besides, I figured that once I quit Lunch Club, I'd never see Jayden again anyway. So I'd be going through all that teasing for nothing.

I mean, Aiden was wrong—I wasn't a genius. But I wasn't stupid, either.

Three A.M.

That night I had this sort-of dream-fantasy:

> I am in a diorama. No, a fish tank. Sort
>   of a crayfish tank, actually.
> And I have everything I need to
>   survive—
> A slice of pizza,
> A sandwich bag of popcorn,
> A scoop of cookie dough ice cream in
>   a cup,
> A tube of cherry ChapStick,

My Life in the Fish Tank

A blue marker,

That super-tiny chair Gabriel gave me,

A sprig of rosemary,

A little covered track to run on,

Maybe some bad movies to watch

    when I get bored,

Although I never do

Because it's cozy in there—

Predictable

And safe.

But the thing is

I can't stop hearing everybody else

Outside the tank

Swimming around

Laughing their heads off,

Making a splash-tsunami—

Shouting faraway words I can barely

    hear.

Thursday

The next day, two extremely weird things happened.

Weird Thing Number One:

Before morning homeroom, I went to Mr. Patrick's office to tell him I was quitting Lunch Club. I knew I could have waited until the following week and just not shown up, but I wanted to be done with the whole thing. Like what they tell you about pulling off a bandage—it hurts less if you yank it off fast. And I knew if I skipped Lunch Club, Mr. Patrick would probably insist on talking to me anyway. I told myself that at least this way, I'd be in charge of when the bandage came off.

But when I got to room 107B, the door was closed.

So I waited outside, fidgeting with my tiny chair thingy, chewing my lip, then smearing on cherry ChapStick, watching kids and teachers rush by on their way to class.

Finally the door opened, and guess who walked out: Kailani. As soon as she saw me, her eyes got huge, and she froze.

ME: Um, hi.

KAILANI: Hi, Zinny! I'm sorry—I didn't know anyone was waiting!

ME: That's okay.

MR. PATRICK *(poking his head out the door and smiling)*: Hey there, Zinny, you wanted to see me?

ME: No, I just . . . it's really not important.

MR. PATRICK: You sure? Because I have some free time now—

KAILANI: Don't worry if you're late for homeroom, Zinny. It doesn't matter. I'll just tell the teacher—

ME: No, yes, I'm sure. Thanks anyway, Mr. Patrick. Um.

And then I raced down the hall to homeroom ahead of Kailani, my heart hammering inside my chest, my brain spinning.

Why was Kailani in Mr. Patrick's office? Was she in there to complain about me—what a bad friend I am, refusing to share secrets and feelings, refusing to apologize to Maisie, saying nasty things about people's crushes?

Or maybe Mr. Patrick was asking her to be a spy, reporting back to him if I yell at people, or won't eat pizza, or something.

I told myself it was possible the conversation was just about Kailani—but she was the kind of person who didn't have problems. At least, not the sort of problems that needed a private meeting with a guidance counselor.

I mean, if you could be any person on earth, you'd be crazy not to pick Kailani.

Weird Thing Number Two:

At dismissal I crashed into Luz. She was blocking the front door of the school with a bunch of eighth graders I didn't know, teen-looking boys and girls, all laughing and yelling insults at one another. From the way the other kids were circled around her, you could tell right away that Luz was popular, maybe the most popular one in the whole group.

Do all these kids know she goes to Lunch Club once a week? And Jayden too?

Luz also had the loudest voice of all the kids, and when my elbow bumped her backpack, she shouted: "Hey!"

I immediately apologized. She gave me a confused look, which was how I realized it hadn't been a *How dare you crash into me* sort of "hey," but more of a *Hello there, I know you* sort of "hey." So I figured this was my chance to thank her for sending us the pizza.

"What pizza?" she asked.

"You know. The one you sent to my house yesterday."

"I didn't send you any pizza. You're the mystery kid, Zin—I don't even know your address!"

"You didn't send it? But the note said Alfredo," I argued.

"Who?"

Now I was blushing. "Remember that joke you made about us being al fresco—"

"Oh right, you mean during Bertha."

"Excuse me?"

"Lunch Club name of the week," Luz whispered behind her hand, as if we were secret agents or something. "Although maybe Jayden sent it. You want to ask him? I saw him here a second ago."

She started looking around in a very obvious way.

Ack. "No, that's okay!"

I grabbed her arm, but she just laughed. "Hey, Jayden! Zin wants to know if you sent her a pizza!"

"Luz, omigod, *please*," I begged.

But too late. Jayden appeared from behind some tall boys.

"Someone sent you pizza, Umzinnia?" he asked, smiling.

I nodded, because I was too embarrassed to form words.

"Well, hate to say it, but it wasn't me," he said. "Although sorry I *didn't* think of it. You never came to Mr. Patrick's office for a slice."

"Yeah, well, I wasn't hungry," I muttered. "After that stupid game we were playing, and everything. Anyhow—"

"So who *did* send it to you, Zin?" Luz traded looks with Jayden. "My guess is Keira."

"Seriously?" I said.

"Yeah, that makes sense, actually," Jayden said. "She felt really bad about what she said."

Luz nodded. "Keira may not seem like it, but she's super sensitive. Maybe we shouldn't tell you this, but afterward she was crying."

Oh, uggghhh. Am I supposed to go thank Keira now? Of all people? Even just having a regular conversation with her was the absolute last thing I felt like doing.

Besides, sending a pizza to my house didn't make up for what she said about Gabriel.

"So you're coming to Bertha next week, right?" Jayden was asking. His dark eyes weren't smiling anymore, and his voice was soft. Serious.

I shrugged.

"Zin, you *have* to," Luz said.

I shrugged again.

Friday, Lunchtime

"Hey there, Zinny," Ms. Molina greeted me from her laptop. She was eating a peanut butter sandwich this time; the smell hit me as soon as I walked into her classroom. But I wasn't hungry; I'd grabbed a hummus wrap from the lunchroom first.

"Any cool plans for the weekend?" She was smiling.

"Not really," I admitted.

"No? Nothing fun going on with friends?"

I rested my backpack on a chair. "Maybe. I guess. I don't know."

"Zinny," Ms. Molina said, putting her sandwich on the

desk. "It's not good to be alone all the time. I used to see you with Kailani and Maisie. What happened between you girls?"

I honestly didn't know how to answer. It wasn't like there was one scientific variable you could point to and say, *Oh, so* that *caused the end of the friendship.* My friendship with Maisie and Kailani just sort of wore out, like an old sneaker.

Sometimes there wasn't a scientific name for things. Or a reason, either.

So I just shrugged.

"Well, what about the kids in Lunch Club?" Ms. Molina asked. "Maybe one of them is free this weekend."

"Yeah, maybe," I said.

To change the subject, I quickly made my way over to the crayfish tanks.

Cray-Z was super active, climbing over pebbles like he was training for the Crustacean Olympics. Crayola was exploring her castle, Ray was swimming, Ashleigh was eating shrimp pellets, while Sugarlumps was sitting on the bottom of the tank, just sort of waving his claws for exercise. As for Clawed, he was hiding.

Although actually . . . where is he, exactly?

Suddenly I had a hollow, icy feeling in my stomach. Like my insides had turned into empty refrigerator shelves.

"Ms. Molina," I called out.

She chewed her sandwich. "Everything okay, Zinny?"

"No," I said. "Clawed isn't here!"

Immediately she was by my side. "Don't worry, he's probably hiding under something. He could be molting; sometimes they hide under things just before they do. I hadn't noticed anything, but—" She stooped to press her face right up against the tank. "Well, that's odd," she finally said.

I searched her face. "He's missing, right?"

"I don't see him," she admitted. "But I know I saw him a little while ago, because I specifically remember thinking how fast he ate his shrimp pellets. . . ."

Ms. Molina's voice trailed as she examined the outside of the tank.

"What are you looking at?" I asked.

"The air-hose line," Ms. Molina said. "It looks a bit displaced."

"What does that mean?"

She slipped her finger under the tube. "It's possible Clawed escaped from the tank. Crayfish are drawn to aeration, so maybe—"

"*He climbed out of the tank?* Through the *air-hose line*?" I squeaked. "But how could he? It's so narrow!"

"It's possible the tank cover wasn't on straight, or there was too much of a gap at the air hose. Crayfish are notorious escape artists; sometimes it's a mystery how they get out! Anyway, the important thing is to find him now, okay? As quickly as possible."

She kept her voice calm and teachery, but I could see worry in her eyes.

The two of us began searching the classroom, not speaking. Ms. Molina focused on tall things—taking books out of the bookshelves in the back of the room—while I crawled around, searching under desks and on the floor of the closet where she kept lab supplies.

Soon kids started trickling in for science class. And of course, as soon as they saw Ms. Molina and me, they knew something was up.

"What's going on?" Aspen demanded.

"All right, folks," Ms. Molina said, wiping her brow with her sleeve. "One of our crayfish guests has escaped his tank. We need everyone to search—"

"Is it Cray-Z?" Li-Mei cried.

"No, it's Clawed."

Aspen shrieked.

Yeah, a lot you care, I thought. *Feeding him hot dogs!*

"Aspen, please stay calm," Ms. Molina said in a no-nonsense sort of way.

"But you said he could dehydrate!" I reminded Ms. Molina. "Don't you remember? And we don't know how long he's been out of the tank, right? So if we don't find him in time, his gills will dry out!"

My voice had a weird, strangled sound. Now everyone was staring at me.

"Zinny," Ms. Molina said, making eye contact. "I'm sure it'll be okay."

"But how *can* you be? Not everything ends up 'okay'!"

"Yes, that's true." Ms. Molina lightly touched my shoulder. "But you're a scientist, Zinny, so think like one: We know how fast Clawed moves, because we have data from your experiment, right? And I know I saw him approximately ten minutes ago. So how far could he have traveled?"

Hot tears filled my eyes, but I blinked them away.

She was asking me to turn this into a science experiment—*be logical, do the math*—when for all we knew, Clawed was in trouble somewhere: a hidden corner we'd never find with math or science.

And the worst part was, deep down I'd always known this would happen. That was why I'd been against the track experiment in the first place! But nobody had listened to me! Not even Ms. Molina.

I dropped to the floor again, peering under tables, garbage cans, chairs. Immediately other people started searching too, and soon the whole class was on their hands and knees.

But I knew we were looking in only the obvious places—and Clawed was sure to be somewhere Not Obvious. Somewhere we wouldn't think to look. Inside a radiator. Between the covers of an observation journal. Or maybe on one of the shelves where Ms. Molina kept her other creatures—the praying mantis, the hissing cockroach. Also all those cacti—

"Clawed," James Ramos called in a singsongy voice. "Claa-aawed, where are you?"

"Don't sing," Darius scolded him. "You'll scare him, dude."

"Maybe we should put out some hot dogs?" Aspen said. "We know he loves the smell."

"Good idea," I blurted. Because it was.

Ms. Molina nodded. "Let me check the mini fridge to see if we have any left over from your experiment."

Suddenly I heard—or thought I heard—a faint scuffling sound behind the *Echeveria elegans*. Before I could think, I reached out and grabbed Clawed off the silvery green succulent—directly behind his claws so he couldn't pinch me—and raced across the room to plop him in his tank.

"Hey, guys, Zinny just found him!" James Ramos yelled.

Ms. Molina beamed at me. "Nice work, Zinny! Now let's all have a look at the tank cover to make sure it's on the right way. We don't want any more escapes!"

"Hey, what's the name of that guy who could escape from anything?" Darius asked.

"You mean Houdini," Li-Mei said.

"Yeah. We should change Clawed's name to that. Houdini."

"No way," Aspen said. "That's like predicting he'll just do it again!"

I burst into tears and ran out of the room.

A Few
Minutes Later

The funny thing was how I ended up in room 107B. I don't remember ever thinking, *Oh, hey, here's an idea— why not see if Mr. Patrick's around?* I mean, I was still planning to quit Lunch Club, and running into Kailani coming out of his office yesterday had definitely freaked me out.

But after the whole Clawed thing, something made me go straight to his office. It could have been knowing he had two boxes of tissues, because I was desperate to wipe my nose.

Anyway, his door was open. He was sitting at his desk typing into his phone, but as soon as I walked in, he looked up.

"Zinny?" he said.

I started crying again.

He shut the door and handed me a whole box of tissues.

"Have a seat," he said, pointing to his lumpy red couch.

I sat.

He sat.

He waited for me to finish crying.

Finally I blew my nose and told him what happened with Clawed. How I'd tried to warn everyone that Clawed would escape, but my group wouldn't listen to me.

"Okay," Mr. Patrick said, "but how would things have been different if your group *had* listened?"

Wasn't it obvious? "Clawed wouldn't have escaped!" I said, still sniffling.

"Are you sure about that, Zinny? Because from what you're telling me, it sounds as if the escape had nothing to do with your track experiment. It sounds as if it was more about the tank itself, and Clawed just being a crayfish, doing standard crayfish things."

I blinked.

"You did nothing wrong," Mr. Patrick said quietly. "This wasn't your fault."

I shrugged.

"There's stuff we can control and stuff we can't. I'd say crayfish behavior belongs in the second category. And you know what, Zinny? Most human behavior does too."

It felt dangerous in the room, like we were teetering on the edge of talking about Gabriel. So before he could say anything else, I told Mr. Patrick I hated Lunch Club.

He didn't seem surprised. "Is this about the game we played?"

"Yeah," I said. "But not only that."

He rubbed his semi-bald head. "Well, I should tell you I've spoken to Keira. She feels terrible, and wants to apologize."

"I don't want her apology. Or her pizza."

"Excuse me?"

"She sent a pizza afterward. To my house."

Mr. Patrick scratched his nose. "Are you sure about that?"

"Well, yeah. I mean, the delivery was from Thom's Pizza—"

"What I'm asking is, are you sure it was Keira?" Now he was smiling.

"Well, who else would it be?" I stared at him. "Was it from you?"

"Actually, no. Not from me."

"Then who?"

"Ah," Mr. Patrick said. "Lunch Club rules forbid me to say."

A Minute after That

So then it was . . . *Asher*?

I mean, it had to be, by the process of elimination. Because it wasn't Mr. Patrick, Luz, Keira, or Jayden.

But why would Asher do a thing like that? He'd never even talked to me. And he barely talked to anyone else, even Luz.

I tried to imagine what had happened—how he'd probably gotten my address from Mr. Patrick, and then called Thom's Pizza to place the order, and told them to write that note: *To Zinny. Because you missed lunch. See you next week, Alfredo.*

Or maybe he wrote the note himself, and handed it to Thom's Pizza.

Either way, it was hard to connect the sulky boy who wouldn't talk to anyone with the person who'd done this really sweet thing.

I couldn't stop my spinning brain. And when I was back upstairs, back in science class, I realized I'd forgotten to quit Lunch Club.

After School on Friday

When the bell rang for dismissal, everyone flew out of school the way they always did on Fridays, headed for sports practice or the Lakeland Diner or their friends' houses or wherever. I spotted Luz and Jayden laughing with all their friends in front of the building, and Kailani talking with Aspen and Li-Mei, and Darius tossing one of those Nerf ball things with James Ramos. And all by himself, walking into town, Asher Hyland.

Crap, I thought.

Because, obviously, I needed to go thank him.

I ran over to him, my heart banging. What if he just

grunted or scowled at me? His scowls were fierce.

"Hey," I said.

He kept walking.

"Hey," I called again, louder this time. I mean, so loud you'd hear even if you had earbuds in, which he did.

He glanced over his shoulder. When he realized it was me who'd called him, he yanked out the earbuds. "Oh," he said, and waited for me to join him.

"I just wanted to thank you—" I began.

"You don't have to," he interrupted.

"Well, but it was really nice of you, Asher. Sending that pizza, I mean. To my house."

I waited for him to deny the whole thing, the way everyone else had. But he didn't. In fact, he didn't say anything. Which was definitely weird, but not in a bad way.

The two of us started walking together, past the drugstore and the barbershop and the nail salon. The whole time his hands were stuffed in his jacket pockets, but he didn't stick his earbuds back in his ears. And he stayed quiet.

All of a sudden he stopped walking. "Can I ask you a question? Do you hate Lunch Club as much as I do?"

"Yeah," I said. "I was going to quit it today. But then I didn't."

"How come?"

"I don't know. I sort of just didn't."

"Yeah, well, *I* almost quit it like five times. No, six." A tiny smile flickered across his face, the first one I'd ever seen. "But I guess I keep forgetting."

"It's not at the top of the list," I said carefully. "With everything else going on."

"Right. For me, too." He looked down at his beat-up sneakers. "Anyway, I guess going to Lunch Club is better than *not* going to Lunch Club."

"That's probably true," I admitted.

"They're the only ones at school who have a clue what it's like. Even *if* they're annoying."

"You think they're annoying? For me it's just Keira."

He raised his eyebrows. "Really? I don't mind her."

"You don't?"

"Nah, she's definitely obnoxious and everything, but at least she's honest. Luz and Jayden both act as if the whole thing is about *them.* Just because they're so popular, and everyone likes them so much, I guess."

I didn't know what to say to that. It sounded like Asher was saying he didn't like Luz and Jayden because they had friends. Which made me wonder if *he* had any. Not that I did at the moment, to be honest.

"And what do you think about Mr. Patrick?" I asked.

"Mr. Patrick is great."

From what I could tell, Asher wasn't a huge compli-menter, so I wasn't sure I'd heard that right. "You mean you *actually like* . . . ?"

"He's the only reason I go to school some days. If I couldn't talk to him about my stepfather, I'd go crazy. Oh," he added, realizing he'd said the word "crazy." "I didn't mean—"

"No, that's okay," I said.

By then we were at Larch Street, where I always turned left. "Asher?" I said. "You want to come over?"

"You mean . . . to your house?"

"Yeah. We could play Minecraft. Or something else—"

"Sure," he said, his face lighting up.

He stuck his hands back in his pockets, not saying another word the rest of the walk home, but I didn't mind.

Ten Minutes Later

As soon as we arrived home, Mom greeted us at the door. She'd just come back from a run, and was still flushed and sweaty, but she chatted with Asher in a very cheerful, normal-mom sort of way. And before we could even take off our jackets, Aiden practically attached himself to Asher's leg, begging to join us while we played Minecraft.

"Yeah, cool," Asher said, as if he really didn't mind.

The three of us sat side by side on the old couch in the TV room, just like we used to do when we watched *My Dog, Drools*. After about an hour Asher admitted he was hungry.

I panicked—did we even have any normal snack food in the house? But when I opened the door of the pantry closet, bags of chips, nuts, and pretzels were lined up on the bottom shelf. Which meant that Mom had gone shopping that afternoon—and not just for basic stuff like microwave dinners and milk.

So then we—Aiden, Asher, and I—sat around munching chips at the dining room table. By this point Asher and I had run out of conversation, so I asked Aiden if he'd had any ideas for his how-to.

Aiden's face fell. "No. And Ms. Felsenstein keeps threatening me."

"*Threatening* you?" Asher asked, frowning.

"He just means his teacher says if he doesn't do a presentation by next week, no more recess," I explained.

"Oh," Asher said, crunching on a chip.

"I keep telling him to keep it simple, but—"

"I *wanted* to do something cool," Aiden interrupted.

"Like what?" Asher asked.

"Like anything! How to Escape If You're Attacked by Leeches! How to Survive Quicksand."

"He needs to demonstrate it," I said, rolling my eyes. "That's the problem."

"Got it," Asher said. He took out his phone and typed something. Then he handed the phone to Aiden. I peeked over my brother's shoulder and read:

How to Make Quicksand:

1. Measure 1 cup of water in a measuring cup. Add to a mixing bowl.

2. Add a couple of drops of food coloring to the water.

3. Add 3 cups of cornstarch to the mixing bowl.

4. Mix with your finger until combined. Then stick your finger in the middle. It's a liquid, right?

5. Give it a punch. Now it feels solid. That's because it's a non-Newtonian fluid—changing its liquidness depending on the force applied to it.

Aiden's eyes popped. "Is this real quicksand? That you can *make*?"

"Why don't you try it?" Asher said, actually grinning at my little brother.

That Night

SCARLETT: Sooooo. I hear a boy came over after school today?

ME: Yep.

SCARLETT: Annnd? Do you *like* him?

ME: He's just my friend, Scar, okay? *Not* a crush or anything. So can you please *not* tease me about it?

SCARLETT: Sure.

ME: Because you know, there's such a thing as a boy *friend*.

SCARLETT: Of course there is.

ME: *Thank* you.

SCARLETT: You're welcome. And you don't need to get so huffy about it, Zinnia.

That Weekend

Aiden made five different batches of quicksand: green, red, blue, brown, yellow. Green was best, he decided, and I didn't bother to challenge him.

He wrote out Asher's directions in his best handwriting, and practiced saying the steps out loud, over and over. Sticking his finger in the middle of the quicksand, then punching it. Saying the word "non-Newtonian."

"This is *so cool*," he kept saying. "Wait till Rudy sees!"

"Who cares about Rudy," I told my brother.

"Me," Aiden said. "I do."

But he was bouncing, and his eyes were shining.

Monday Morning

With all the stuff he had to carry for his How to Make Quicksand demonstration, Mom drove Aiden to school, the first time she hadn't made him take the bus since late November. So I was feeling pretty happy as I walked to school—happy that Mom was returning to Mom behavior. Happy that Aiden finally had a cool project. Happy that I'd made friends with Asher Hyland, of all people. Even happy that I hadn't let Scarlett tease me about it.

Also, for the first time in weeks, not even caring that I was walking alone.

But half a block from school, someone shouted my name. And then Keira was at my side, panting.

"You walk too fast," she complained.

"Sorry," I said.

Her face puckered. "Can we talk, Zinny? I'm really sorry—"

"You don't have to apologize." It was funny, but I meant it. The whole Mad-Sad-Glad game suddenly seemed like months ago. *Abnormal Standard Time,* I thought.

Keira shook her head. "Okay, Zinny, but I *want* to apologize. I *know* I have a stupid big mouth, all right? But after my sister told me about your brother, I just thought everyone knew—"

I froze. "Your *sister*?"

"Yeah, my big sister Jocelyn. She goes to school with your sister. Scarlett," she added, as if I didn't know the name of my own sister.

"Wait," I said slowly. "You heard about my brother from your sister? Because Scarlett *told* her . . . ?"

"Well, no. Scarlett didn't tell *my sister*, specifically. She's just been talking about it a lot at their school. To everyone. You know, like 'Don't give me any crap today, because my brother went crazy and smashed up a car.'"

"Keira, stop," I begged. "Please."

"I'm just incredibly sorry," Keira said quickly. "For everything I said to you, Zinny, okay? About being mad at your brother. And him doing it on purpose. And I'm also really sorry he's so sick—"

"You don't need to be. He's doing great," I said, running away from her, into the building.

Right after That

My brain was spinning:

> Scarlett is telling everyone about
>   Gabriel!
> Even though Mom and Dad said we
>   shouldn't!
> Why would she do that?
> What right did she have?
> Because it's my secret too!
> Unless . . . unless it isn't even a secret
>   anymore.

And what I did just now—
telling Keira he's "doing great"—
how is that different from lying?
It isn't.

Not knowing where else to go, I went straight to room 107B.

"So does the whole school know?" I asked the second I was inside the door.

Mr. Patrick looked up at me from his desk chair. "About what, Zinny?" he asked.

"My brother Gabriel. That he's bipolar. That he's in a residential treatment center." My heart was banging, and my voice was hoarse. "That he went crazy and smashed up somebody's car. And hurt himself. Maybe on purpose."

Mr. Patrick motioned for me to sit on the lumpy red sofa. I hadn't meant to have a whole long conversation about this, but right at that moment, Asher's words ("Mr. Patrick is great") were echoing in my head.

Also, my legs were shaking.

So I sat.

Mr. Patrick closed his office door.

"I don't know, Zinny, is the answer to your question," he

said, taking his seat again. "I know Keira heard about it through her big sister, because she mentioned it to me. But I haven't heard anything like that from other kids here at school. May I ask why you're wondering?"

I told him what Keira had said, how Scarlett was blabbing to everyone at the high school, disobeying my parents.

"Well." Mr. Patrick rubbed his cheek. "I guess I can understand the different sides here. Why your parents asked you to keep this information private, but also why your sister wanted to talk about it. How do *you* feel about it, Zinny?"

Uggghhh, here we go again. That question. "I don't know! A million ways!"

"Tell me three."

"Mad. Tired. Worried." Then I heard myself say: "Ashamed."

He smiled a little. "That's four."

"Yeah. Well, I said a million, so."

"You did. And I want you to know that all your feelings— all million of them—are *completely okay*. There's no right way to feel about it, and no wrong way either."

I chewed my lower lip.

He watched me for a few seconds. Then he said in a

gentle voice, "But let me ask about the last word you said—
'ashamed.' Where does that come from?"

"I don't know," I muttered. "Not everyone has a crazy
brother."

"I thought you said he was bipolar."

"Yeah, he is."

"So that's a specific treatable medical condition. Let's
try to avoid the word 'crazy.'"

"Okay. Not everyone has a brother *in a mental hospital*,"
I corrected myself.

"But you said Gabriel is in a residential treatment center. *Not* a hospital, right?"

I nodded.

"The right words are important, Zinny," Mr. Patrick
said quietly. "As a scientist, you should know that. Are you
ashamed that he's getting help?"

"No, but—"

"If he were being treated for cancer or heart problems,
would you be ashamed of that?"

"No, of course not. But mental illness is different."

"Why?"

"It just is. People make fun of it."

"Because they don't understand." Mr. Patrick sat all the

way forward in his chair. "I guess the question is: Why worry about those people, when there are so many other people who really care about you?"

"Like who?"

"I can name you a million." He started counting on his fingers. "Let's see: Lunch Club, which is four great kids. Ms. Molina. Me. Your friend Kailani—"

I grunted. "She's not my friend anymore."

Mr. Patrick smiled as if he had a secret. "Not what I hear," he said.

Monday, Tuesday, Wednesday

Talking to Mr. Patrick that Monday morning calmed me down a little. As the day went by (math quiz, fire drill, volleyball in gym), I decided not to yell at Scarlett for blabbing. The more I thought about it, the less sure I felt that Mom and Dad were right. Maybe what happened to Gabriel shouldn't have been a secret in the first place. Not only because it felt bad to be—or even *seem* to be—ashamed of him, but also because I knew secrets had a way of getting out, no matter how hard you tried to keep them inside. Sort of like crayfish escaping from tanks—you just knew it was going to happen, sooner or later.

And I thought that maybe everything at school, all the problems with Maisie and Kailani, might not have happened if I'd talked to them a little.

Not that I *wanted* to talk about Gabriel, obviously. The whole thing hurt my heart in a way I couldn't describe—to them, or the Lunch Club kids, or anyone else, even Mr. Patrick. Gabriel was special to me, my big brother with the Christmas-tree smile, and I couldn't explain to anyone how it felt to wonder if he'd be okay. And I still definitely didn't want conversations in the lunchroom, in front of everyone. But maybe thinking that I *could* talk about it if I wanted to would have changed things.

Maybe. Maybe not.

I spent the next two days peeking at Kailani, noticing how she sat with Li-Mei in homeroom, walked to classes with Priya Patel, ate lunch with James Ramos. (I knew this because I had lunch both days with Asher, although at the end of lunch on Tuesday, we went to visit Ms. Molina's lab. "Always happy to have you bring your friends," Ms. Molina told me, emphasizing the word "friends.")

As for Maisie, she seemed to be talking to Aspen. Hardly anyone else. Whatever that meant.

Even so, I didn't say anything to Kailani. The last real

conversation we'd had was so weird, and felt so long ago. Besides, I couldn't think of anything to say. *Hey, remember all that time I refused to talk to you? Well, I'm ready now. Aren't you happy?*

And then it was time for Lunch Club.

LUZ: Behold, earthlings! I made cupcakes for Asher's birthday!

ASHER *(blushing)*: Oh God.

ME: It's your birthday? Happy birthday, Asher!

ASHER: Ugh. Can we *please* not—

LUZ: Sorry, Asher, we're celebrating the day you arrived on this planet! This is not a choice!

ASHER: *(covers his head with his arms, groans)*

KEIRA: Those cupcakes are kind of smashed-looking. And blue icing is kind of weird.

JAYDEN: Who cares! I bet they taste great!

LUZ: Yeah, bro, they do! I had a couple last night. Under the icing they're *chocolate*.

MR. PATRICK: This was incredibly sweet of you, Luz. Wait a sec, I know where they have candles in the faculty room. *(Runs out of room 107B.)*

ASHER *(blushing, smiling)*: Listen, I'll blow out a candle

and make a wish *if* you guys promise not to sing "Happy Birthday."

ME: Deal.

LUZ: Hey, I didn't say *I* agreed—

ME: *Deal.* Okay, Luz?

LUZ *(grinning)*: Whatever, Zin.

MR. PATRICK *(returns with one yellow candle, sticks it in cupcake)*: Success!

JAYDEN: Hey, Mr. P, we've taken a vote, and we're not singing "Happy Birthday."

MR. PATRICK: Cool. I've always hated that song anyway. *(Lights candle.)*

(Asher thinks for a few seconds, blows candle out. Everyone cheers.)

Pizza arrived.

We stuffed ourselves with pizza and cupcakes.

We talked about nothing:

A stupid YouTube video of kittens with balloons.

Luz's new guinea pig named Trouble.

The time Jayden got stuck at the top of a Ferris wheel and distracted himself by singing *Hamilton*.

A video game Asher's mom got him for his birthday.

It was great, like a regular birthday party. Everyone was smiling. Even Asher.

MR. PATRICK: Okay, folks, for the last ten minutes, why don't we do a little catching up—

KEIRA: Aww, do we *have* to? This was *fun*.

ASHER: *And* it's my birthday.

MR. PATRICK: Fine, Asher, I'll go easy on you today. Keira, how was the week with your mom?

KEIRA: All right, I guess. No major freak-outs.

MR. PATRICK: Good to hear. And Jayden?

JAYDEN: My dad saw the doctor yesterday. Everything's the same.

MR. PATRICK: Same is awesome. We like the same. *(Fist-bumps Jayden.)* Luz?

LUZ: Okay, so last night I had a big long talk with my mom about the checking-up-on-me stuff. She was really upset at first, and she started acting all emotional, but I think she got my feelings by the end. I *hope*!

ME: That's so cool that you could talk to her like that.

LUZ: Yeah, talking is never my problem, haha! What about you?

ME *(heart stopping)*: Me?

LUZ: Yeah, did you ever talk to your friends? About that apology stuff you were telling us about?

ME *(heart beating again)*: Oh, that. No, I kind of gave up on those friends, I guess.

LUZ: Well, but you shouldn't, Zin, you know? How are you going to work stuff out if you just give up on people?

ME:

Wednesday, after School

I rang Kailani's doorbell. She didn't answer right away; I thought I saw her peeking out from behind the curtain. Finally the door opened.

"Hey," she said softly.

"Hey," I said. "I've been thinking about Tulip and Daffodil, and I realized I haven't seen them in forever. Can I come in?"

"Oh, sure," she said. But she didn't sound sure. For a second a thought flashed in my mind: Was Maisie here too? If she was, I could still turn and run.

I followed Kailani into the sunny kitchen. A very old

woman was sitting at the table with a pink plastic bib around her neck, eating orange Jell-O.

"Nana, this is my friend Zinny," Kailani said loudly.

The old woman stared at me. A bit of Jell-O glistened on her chin.

"You want a snack?" Kailani asked me politely.

My stomach was still full of pizza and cupcake, so I told her no thanks.

Kailani leaned into her grandma's face. "Nana, we're going into the living room for a minute. I'll be able to hear if you need anything. Okay, Nana?"

The woman blinked at her.

"That's your grandma?" I whispered as Kailani and I walked down the hall.

"Yes, she's been living with us since her stroke last month. It's been really hard to see her like this. And not be able to do anything about it."

"Oh, I'm sorry," I said. "I didn't know."

"Well, Zinny, you have your own stuff going on."

"Yeah, I do, but." A hot wave of shame passed over me. Thinking Kailani had zero problems had been really unfair to her. Maybe she hadn't been the best friend in the world, but neither had I, actually.

"Let me find Tulip and Daffy," Kailani was saying. "Oh, there's Tulip under the chair. Come out, silly." Kailani scooped up the droopy black cat and nuzzled her head. She put Tulip down again, the whole time talking without looking in my direction. "But where's Daffy? She's gotten so fat she hardly moves lately! Probably she's on my bed."

I followed Kailani up the stairs to her small bedroom. Daffodil had spread herself all over Kailani's pillow, and Kailani immediately buried her face in Daffodil's fur, cooing the silly, soothing things people say to cats: "You sneaky girl, did you think you were hiding from me? Of course I'd find you!"

All of a sudden it seemed Kailani was hiding from *me*. Not that I could blame her.

I took a deep breath. "Kailani?" I said. "Can we please talk a second?"

She kept her face in Daffodil's fur. "About what? You said you wanted to see the cats—"

"No, I wanted to see *you*."

"Oh. Well, here I am."

Weird pause.

"Kailani, are you still friends with Maisie?" I blurted.

She finally sat up and looked at me. "Not . . . exactly."

"What happened?"

"You really want to hear?"

I nodded.

Kailani blew out some air. "Well, Zinny, when you were being so weird with us, not talking about *anything*, I got worried, so I went to see Mr. Patrick. That's how you got invited to that Lunch Club thing. And when I finally told Maisie about it, she got mad at *me*. Like she thought I went behind her back."

"That's crazy," I said. Then I corrected myself. "I mean, not *crazy*, but wrong."

"I know."

"And how come Maisie was so against me doing Lunch Club, anyway? I mean, I remember she said her sister didn't like it, but—"

"She thinks those kids are weird. Especially Asher and Keira."

"Well, they are, a bit." I smiled. "But they're also nice."

"Anyhow, I think she always felt a little jealous about our friendship, how the two of us were friends first. And you know how she likes organizing everybody, so she got mad when we didn't do what she wanted. But now I'm not friends with either of you anymore, which is so unfair, because all I did was try to help. . . ." Kailani's voice was trembling.

"Kailani, I'm still your friend," I said quickly.

"You are?"

I sat on the bed and ruffled Daffodil's soft fur. "Of course I am. I know you kept asking how I felt because you cared about me. But I couldn't talk about it; I'm really sorry."

"Zinny, you don't have to apologize—"

"No, I think I do. And thanks for going to Mr. Patrick. The Lunch Club is pretty good. Even if I don't always want to go."

"You mean that?"

I nodded. "But I'm still mad that you stopped walking with me."

"Oh, and I'm mad at me too! For letting Maisie boss me around like that! But you kept on pushing me away, so it was just easier to go along with her, you know? Anyhow, I'm so, so sorry about it, Zinny! Do you forgive me?"

"Yeah. Do you forgive me for pushing you away?"

She held out her arms, and we hugged for like an entire minute.

Then Daffodil reached across the pillow to scratch my hand.

Thursday Supper, Friday Afternoon

At first Aiden couldn't stop talking about what a hit his presentation was that day, how all the kids kept punching the green quicksand until finally Ms. Felsenstein had to take the bowl and stick it on a high shelf. Even Rudy called Aiden's quicksand project "super cool," Aiden said. Plus, Rudy played with Aiden at recess, which he hadn't done in like a year.

As we all ate penne, broccoli, and turkeyballs, Aiden's cheeks were pink and his eyes glowed. It was great to see my little brother so proud of himself, and so happy. *Wait until I tell Asher,* I thought.

But all of a sudden Aiden announced that he wasn't hungry and that his head hurt.

"Probably from the excitement," Mom said, smiling. "Come over here, baby." She leaned over and kissed his forehead.

Then she frowned. "You're a little warm," she told him. "Does anything else feel funny?"

Aiden nodded. "My throat."

Mom and Dad looked at each other.

"You'd better not be getting sick, Aid," Dad said. "Because we're supposed to be driving up to see Gabriel this weekend."

"No problem, you guys can still go," Scarlett said. "I'll take care of Aiden."

"Scarlett, you can't," Mom said.

"Why not?" Scarlett demanded.

"Because you don't know how."

"So just tell me what to do, and I'll do it!"

Yeah, right, I thought. *Because you always follow orders, Scarlett.*

"Anyhow, I'm not even sick," Aiden promised.

By Friday morning, it was clear that he was sick— feverish and sniffly. Mom said she'd take him to the doctor, and when I came home from school, I was bet-ting we wouldn't be driving up to Redwoods Village.

But Mom said she'd called her friends Carrie and Son-dra, and between the two of them popping in, and Scarlett being home with full instructions, she felt sure we could still visit Gabriel for Saturday. "And you know he's expect-ing us," she told me. "It's important to be consistent."

It sounded like something she'd read on a website: *How to Survive If Your Kid Is Bipolar.*

"But what about me?" I asked.

Mom looked at me, confused. "What do you mean?"

I swallowed. "If Scarlett isn't going, and Aiden won't need babysitting at Redwoods Village, what am *I* supposed to do up there the whole time?"

Mom stroked my hair. "Sweetheart, Dad and I talked it over, and we think this time it would be wonderful if you joined us in the session."

I wasn't sure I'd heard that right. "You mean be in Gabriel's therapy?"

She nodded. "I know he'd appreciate it, Zinny, and so would Dad and I. It's really intended for the whole family—"

"But why do I have to do it if Scarlett doesn't? And Aiden?"

"Aiden is too young," Mom replied.

"Okay, what about Scarlett?"

"We're working on that," Mom said crisply. "Go get packed now, Zinny, okay?"

I let out a big sigh—more of a groan, really—and stomped off to my bedroom.

Scarlett was sitting on her bed, watching as I tossed some pj's and underwear in my overnight bag. I didn't say anything, and I guess she noticed.

"So are you mad at me?" she asked softly.

I shrugged. "Yeah. You should be visiting Gabriel, Scarlett."

Her face flushed. "Well, *of course* I can't! Aiden is sick! Someone has to be home to watch him—"

"That's not the only reason you aren't coming. It's like you're afraid of it, Scar. Is that why you keep talking about it at school? Because you're afraid?"

Scarlett's mouth dropped open. And I think it wasn't just because she was shocked that I knew about her telling everyone at school. I think it was also because it wasn't a little-sister sort of thing to say.

Like I'd pushed her off a step, or something.

"Well, sure I'm afraid," she said in a small voice. "Aren't you, Zinny?"

"Yeah," I said. "I am. We all are. But I bet Gabriel is too."

Saturday at
Redwoods Village

"I'm glad you came, Zinny," Gabriel said as he poured maple syrup on a waffle. "But too bad Aiden is sick."

"Just a cold," Mom said. "He'll be fine in a couple of days. Zinny, tell Gabriel about your crayfish experiment."

To be honest, I didn't want to—I doubted Gabriel would be interested. But at least it gave me something to talk about. And the whole time I was talking, Gabriel was listening. He'd gotten a haircut, so you could see his eyes.

He looked . . . okay. Like Gabriel, really.

I could feel my shoulders relax.

Then Dad took a sip of coffee and said it was time for the family therapy session. "We thought Zinny would join us this week," he said.

"Yeah?" Gabriel said, like he was doubtful or something.

My stomach knotted.

The four of us walked down a long, beige-carpeted hallway to a small room with five wooden chairs and one of those tall potted plants you usually see only in dentist offices. Near the plant was a small square table with a box of tissues. On the walls were big framed paintings—seascapes, landscapes. Nowhere I could identify. They gave me the shivers.

We each picked a chair and sat down in this order: Mom, Gabriel, Dad, me.

The overhead lights buzzed.

Nothing happened.

"She's never late," Mom explained to me. "We're a minute early."

"You're always early for everything," Gabriel said.

I eyed him. Was that a complaint? Was that what this "session" was about—complaining about each other?

Would Gabriel have a complaint about *me*?

I rubbed on some ChapStick.

The door opened. A small Black woman with waist-long braids and a heavy-looking turquoise necklace padded in. She wore an ankle-length plain blue dress, sort of like an overgrown sweatshirt, and ballet flats, and as she shook everyone's hands, her feet swished against the carpeting.

"I'm Gabriel's psychologist, Dr. Imani Watkins," she told me. She had a bright, clear voice and a sweet smile. "You can call me Imani, if you like."

"Okay," I murmured.

"Well, I'm delighted to finally meet you. Gabe's told me so much about you," she said, still smiling.

I looked at Gabriel. He shrugged, almost like he was embarrassed.

The session started. Imani talked a bunch about Gabriel's medicines—which she called "meds"—and Mom and Dad asked questions about dosage and interactions. Once in a while Gabriel added something, but I couldn't follow any of this conversation, to be honest, and I started to wonder what I was even doing there. So I just sat fingering the tiny chair Gabriel had given me, zipped up in my hoodie pocket. And staring at the nowhere-scapes, trying to imagine why anyone would paint them.

After about ten minutes, Imani turned to me and

smiled. "So, Zinny," she said. "This session is meant to be a conversation. Would you like to ask your brother any questions?"

This startled me. I wasn't prepared—I had nothing *but* questions, really. *Will you ever be coming home? Were you trying to hurt yourself—kill yourself—with the car? How come you never told us you needed help?* But as I sat in this small room with the buzzing light, my brain had logged out.

I shook my head.

"Zinny has been so great through this whole thing," Dad said. "Such a huge help at home. Especially with her brother Aiden."

"That's wonderful," Imani said, nodding.

"Zinny, tell Imani about Aiden's how-to project," he said.

I squirmed in the chair. How much did Dad know about Aiden's project? More than I'd realized, apparently.

"I'd rather not talk about it," I said. "It's kind of long."

"Well, your parents are clearly very proud of you, Zinny," Imani said. "How does it make you feel to hear that?"

"Okay," I said, sliding my index finger around the tiny chair thingy.

"Just okay?" She kept her eyes on me.

Everyone was watching me, waiting for me to speak, but

I couldn't. All I wanted was to escape—and if there'd been an aeration tube somewhere in the ceiling, I'd have figured out a way to crawl out.

"Zinny?" Imani said in a soothing voice, the kind you'd use to lure a cat hiding under the sofa. "Can you tell us what you're feeling right now?"

UGGGHHH. That question again. Everybody watching, waiting for my answer.

"Mad," I blurted.

Mom's face crumpled.

"Not just mad," I said immediately. "Also sad. It's not one thing."

"Can you explain, Zinny?" Imani asked gently.

"Just, I don't know! I wish I weren't here." I took a breath. "I wish we were all home, and everything was back the way it used to be. And that our whole family wasn't only about *this* all the time!"

Dead silence in the room, except for the buzzing.

"Yeah, me too," Gabriel said. "Absolutely."

Something made me keep going. "And you know what else I wish more than *anything*? That this whole thing wasn't a big secret!"

Gabriel stared at me. "What are you talking about?"

"We're not supposed to tell people about it! About *you*."

Gabriel's eyes filled with tears. He didn't say anything for a second. Then he turned to Mom and Dad. "How come?" His voice broke. "Why would you say that to her? Is that what you told Scar and Aiden?"

"Sweetheart, please don't be upset," Mom said quickly. "We just thought with everything you were going through, you'd want some privacy—"

"Well, I *don't*," Gabriel said. "This is my *life*, Mom. From now on! And I don't want Zinny, or anyone else in the family, acting like there's something to *hide* about it! Like there's something to be ashamed about!"

"We're not ashamed," Mom cried out. "Oh, Gabe, how can you say that?"

Yes, he's doing well. All healed up and back at college. Studying dinosaurs—

Gabriel's face was red. "Mom, are you seriously asking me this? Because that's *exactly* how it seems!"

"Sweetheart, please—"

"You're right," Dad said all of a sudden.

Mom shot him a look of disbelief. "*Eric.* I thought we agreed—"

But Dad kept talking to Gabriel in a strange, choky

voice. "Mom and I were just trying to think about *you*, what you wanted, Gabe. What you needed from us. But we should have asked *you*. We were wrong. And please believe me, I'm—we're both—very sorry."

Dad covered his face and his shoulders shook. I was so used to Mom's way of crying that at first I didn't realize Dad was crying—but he was, even though he made no noise. I'd never seen him cry before this minute, and it gave me a hollow feeling inside. Kind of a bottom-step-collapsing sort of feeling.

Then, not looking up, Dad reached out his hand, and Gabriel grabbed it.

Mom burst into loud, wet sobs and threw her arms around Gabriel. "Me too," she said. "Oh, me too! I'm so, so sorry, baby."

"It's okay, Mom," Gabriel murmured, not letting go of Dad's hand.

Now my throat ached and my eyes were stinging. And what was I supposed to do? Get up and join the teary hug? It was about Gabriel forgiving Mom and Dad, not me.

But it felt weird just to sit there. So I went over and threw my arms around them. We stayed like that for a minute or two.

When I sat back down, I glanced at Imani, whose eyes were closed. *Maybe,* I thought, *she was giving us all privacy. She's probably used to stuff like this. Definitely more than I am.* Anyway, I thanked her in my mind for not watching.

When Mom finally took her seat again, Imani passed around the box of tissues. "It's very good that we were able to get that out in the open. Thank you, Zinny, for sharing that. I feel like we're making so much real progress here."

Mom blew her nose. "Speaking of progress, Imani. When will Gabriel be coming home, do you think?"

"That's a decision for the medical doctors. But as Gabriel knows, at this point we've been discussing July as a realistic goal."

Mom let out a squeal. Dad coughed into his tissue.

July wasn't soon—but it was a page on the calendar. You could even turn to it and see the Rescue Dog of the Month.

My eyes filled with happy tears.

Then Imani started another speech about the schedule for Gabriel's therapy. I couldn't make sense out of it—and I didn't need to. All I needed to know was one word: *July.*

A word that was Normal Standard Time.

July, July, July.

Monday, Lunch Period

At lunch, I had the idea of bringing Kailani and Asher to visit the crayfish. Part of this was to let Kailani see how nice Asher was, once you got to know him. Also, I wanted Ms. Molina to see that Kailani and I were friends again. Real friends, even better than before.

So the three of us got sandwiches from the lunchroom and brought them upstairs to her lab. Ms. Molina was at her laptop, a bit distracted, I thought, but she still showed Asher and Kailani all the cool stuff: the hissing cockroach, the shark teeth, the best cacti, and all seven of the crayfish. (Ashleigh was molting, so we spent the rest of the period just watching her.)

When the bell rang, Ms. Molina tapped my arm. "Zinny, can I speak to you privately?"

"Sure," I said.

I said good-bye to Asher and Kailani.

My teacher closed the door. "Don't worry, this is good news," she explained quickly. "I just heard from Blue Shoals Marine Lab, and you got in."

I stared at her, not understanding. "You mean to that summer program?"

"Yes," Ms. Molina said. "Exactly."

I screamed and jumped. Ms. Molina laughed.

"It's going to be so fantastic," she said. "The best summer ever. Here, look." She turned her laptop so I could see.

Welcome to the Blue Shoals Marine Lab summer program for highly motivated middle schoolers! This year, our celebrated program runs four weeks, from July 13 to August 7.

July.

July, July, July.

"Oh," I said.

Ms. Molina smiled into my face. "Sounds awesome, right? You can't believe it?"

"I can't go."

"What? Why can't you?"

"I just . . . have something else to do," I said.

"What is it?"

"I can't talk about it," I said.

Although now I could, because it wasn't a secret any-more.

But it was still too much to explain.

Rest of the Spring

That was the last time I went to Ms. Molina's lab during lunch.

Now I had kids to eat lunch with—Kailani, Asher, Keira. Sometimes we ate with Li-Mei, Priya, and even James Ramos (who, it turned out, actually did have a crush on Kailani). And a few times Maisie joined us. We weren't going to be friends again, not like before, but we were okay enough to eat lunch at the same table, which was a big relief.

Besides, in science class one day, Ms. Molina announced that she'd be packing up all the tanks and sending off the crayfish. To visit another school twenty miles away, she said.

So I told myself there was no point, anyway.

The Last
Weekend of School

School ended with two big parties—one at Li-Mei's house, one at Jayden's. I went to both—even though Jayden's made me nervous, because, except for Asher and Keira, it was all eighth graders, ecstatic about their graduation from middle school.

Jayden even danced with me once. (I knew it didn't mean anything—he was so popular that like five other girls danced with him first—but I also told myself it didn't mean *nothing*. Maybe.)

Anyhow, when the music ended, the two of us walked over to the pizza table, where Keira, Luz, and Asher were arguing about toppings. "Sorry, but pineapple does *not* belong on pizza," Luz was saying.

"How can you say that if you haven't even tried it?" Keira shouted.

"I don't *have* to try it to know it's just *wrong*! Some things are so completely obvious! What do you think, Zin?"

"Me?" I said. "I've never even thought about pineapple on pizza."

"Well, think about it now!" Keira said. "We demand you take a side!"

I chose a slice of pizza with pepperoni. "I think everyone should eat whatever they like. But they should also try new things, even if, truthfully, it sounds disgusting."

"Thanks?" Keira stuck her tongue out at me.

"Well, *I* think Zinny gave the perfect answer," Jayden said.

"So do I," Asher said, smiling. (I mean, smiling for Asher.) "Anyhow, it's a stupid argument."

"We're aware it's *stupid*," Keira informed him. "That's kind of the *point*, Asher."

I looked at the four of them.

"You know what?" I blurted. "I think I'm going to miss our stupid arguments."

Luz patted my back. "Never fear, Zin, there is definitely more Eunice in your future."

"*Eunice?*" Keira said, laughing. "That's the best name yet!"

"Thank you." Luz grinned. "Anyway, my point is you guys can't escape Lunch Club. Mr. Patrick will hunt you down."

"He will," Jayden agreed. "So the three of you can keep stupid-arguing all you want. And Luz and I aren't disappearing—we'll just be over at the high school." He smiled at me. "So anyway . . . what are you doing this summer, Umzinnia?"

"Me?" I took a small bite of pizza.

"Yes, you," Luz said. "And you're not squirming out of this question either."

They watched as I chewed the pepperoni.

"Um," I said. "Well, actually, I think I'll be hanging out with my brother."

"You mean Aiden?" Asher asked.

"No, my older brother. Gabriel." I put down the pizza and wiped my mouth with a napkin. Then I said, "He's been away at a residential treatment center for this mental illness he has—bipolar disorder—but he's ready to come home now, so. I think he'll need help, maybe, I don't know. Or just company."

"That's really great, Zinny," Asher said quietly. "That he's coming home, and everything."

"Yeah, it is." Jayden looked at me with his beautiful eyes.

"Thanks for telling us," Keira said, not adding the word "finally."

Luz just threw her arms around me and squeezed tight.

Middle of June/Early July

And snap: now it was summer.

Scarlett was bagging groceries at Ellman's Market, Aiden was going to town camp with Rudy, and my plan was to walk neighborhood dogs to earn some money. That and hang out with my friends. But mostly with Gabriel, who would be coming home on July 2.

Although first Mom and Dad decided our house needed painting—so for the last few days of June, we all helped. Aiden chose blue for his room, and Scarlett and I chose a sunny yellow. Gabriel said he wanted his room painted white—it just seemed clean, he said, like a fresh start.

"Okay," Mom said, "but don't you want maybe a *little* color?"

"No," he said firmly. "Besides, I won't be there very much when I go back to college."

Mom didn't answer. I wondered if that meant Gabriel was actually returning to school in the fall, or if Mom just didn't want a big argument.

Or just *that* big argument.

A few days later Mom and I were in the garden, picking some lavender. Mom had this idea that she wanted to make little silk bags of dried herbs—sachets, she called them—to give to Imani and some of the staff at Redwoods Village who had helped Gabriel these past six months.

"And one for Ms. Molina, too," she added. "As a thank-you. Not just for giving us all these herbs, but also for nominating you for that special program."

"Yeah, well," I said uncomfortably. "Actually, I'm not doing that program."

She looked up at me. "But Ms. Molina told us you got in."

"Yeah, I did. I've just been thinking that . . . I'd rather be home this summer. With our whole family."

With Gabriel, I meant. But probably that was obvious.

Mom exhaled slowly. "That's fine, sweetheart, if it's really what you want. No one's forcing you to go. But can I tell you something I've learned in therapy? Whatever's going on with Gabriel, it's important for us—our whole family—to keep doing the stuff we care about. All the things that make us who we are." She brushed my arm with a bunch of lavender. "Including funny-looking sea creatures."

I decided not to point out that crayfish weren't *sea creatures*. "Maybe, but what about you, Mom? You care about being a teacher, right? So when are you going back to work?"

"September." Mom was smiling now. Her face still looked tired, but it was her regular smile. "After the summer, I'll be teaching eleventh grade again. And I can't wait."

On July 2, Mom and Dad drove to Redwoods Village to bring Gabriel home.

I stayed behind to make welcome-home cupcakes, because it seemed like we should celebrate. So I made Luz's recipe: chocolate, with a big blue *G* on every one.

Mom, Dad, and Gabriel arrived home in the evening. Mom and Dad looked exhausted when they got out of the car, but Gabriel seemed happy to be back. Scarlett told him all about her road test (which, yay, she'd passed) and this boy she liked who Gabriel knew. Aiden wouldn't shut up about some video game he'd heard about from Rudy.

Gabriel ate two cupcakes and kissed my cheek.

"Tomorrow we'll go to Here's the Scoop," he told me. "And we'll get Monster Cones, okay?"

"I wanna come too!" Aiden wailed.

"Next time, buddy," Gabriel said, mussing his hair. "Tomorrow it's just me and Zinny."

I felt so happy it was like I was made of light molecules. Like I was swimming through bubbly water.

"Yeah, well, I'm driving," Scarlett informed him loudly.

July 3

Just like Gabriel said we would, the next day we went to Here's the Scoop.

And Scarlett drove us. "I'm not even jealous of you guys," she announced as we entered the parking lot. "I don't even feel the *teeniest* bit left out."

"You can join us if you want," I said.

"Nah, I have work, and afterward I'm going over to Jamilla's. Anyway, tomorrow Gabe and I are taking the red wagon out for a spin, and you can't play with us, Zinnia. *Joking*," she added, sticking her tongue out at me.

All three of us laughed so loudly a woman in the parking

lot gave us a dirty look. *The Manning kids have a reputation for noisiness. And splash fights.*

Just before she drove off, Scarlett said Mom would pick us up in an hour.

Gabriel winked at me. "Think they'll ever trust me with the car again?"

"Nope," I said.

"Oof, that hurts." He pretended to clutch his chest and stagger, as if I'd wounded him.

"Sorry," I said. "I just meant it will take a while—"

"No, I totally get it. I'm teasing you, Monkeygirl."

I grinned. We both ordered Monster Cones and took them to a tiny table in the back.

"So what's going on with you?" he asked. "I mean, for the summer."

"Not much. I may walk dogs—"

"Boring."

I licked my spoon. "Well, at least I'll earn some money."

He was watching my face. "What about that summer program Mom was talking about? The science one. You didn't get in?"

"No, I did."

"Then why aren't you going? It's too expensive?"

"No, it's free."

"Soooo?" He blinked. "Why are you sitting here, then?"

"Because . . ." I couldn't finish.

Gabriel nodded once, slowly. "*Oh*. You mean because of *me*."

I ate some ice cream.

"Zinny," he said. "If you think I'm going to let you sit around and stare at me all summer, you're crazy. And *I'm* the crazy one in this family, not you."

"You're not crazy. You're bipolar." I swallowed some hot fudge. "And I'm not going to stare at you, Gabriel."

"You'd better not." He laughed. "Seriously, though, you don't need to worry about me. Or take care of me, if that's what you thought you'd be doing." He looked straight into my eyes. "I'm pretty good now, actually."

I leaned across the table toward him. "You really are? You *swear*, Gabriel?"

"Yeah." He caught a drip of fudge with his finger. "I mean, *obviously* I have to stay on top of my meds, and I'll be seeing doctors and doing therapy for the rest of my life, probably. But as long as I watch my routine and exercise and stress level and all that kind of stuff, and just stay *aware* of everything, I really think I'll be okay."

"And you won't . . . ?" I couldn't finish the sentence, but I could tell Gabriel knew what I meant.

"Zinny, all I can promise is that if I'm having trouble again, I'll get help. I know I can do that now, and I will. You believe me?"

How could I not? After all this time, here we were again, just the two of us. Finally talking.

"Yeah, I believe you," I said softly.

"Good." He exhaled a little. "And you know, I'm *definitely* going back to school in the fall."

"You are? Do Mom and Dad know? I mean, you told them?"

"Yep. They're both nervous about it, but they'll be fine." Gabriel took a bite of ice cream. "Mom's going back to school too, actually."

"Yeah, she told me. I'm really glad."

He nodded. "So you see, you got your wish, Zin: we're not just about *this* anymore." He drew a little circle in the air with his spoon. "Now stop worrying about everyone, and go off this summer and do something about *you*, okay?"

I looked at him, really looked at him then. His clear hazel eyes. His glowing smile. He looked like Gabriel again. Like my big brother.

But.

"I can't," I told him. "I mean, I already told them no, so it's probably too late. And anyhow, the program starts this month."

"Don't be so negative, Monkeygirl," he said. He tapped my shoulder, like he was poking me with an invisible wand. "Hey, you still have that miniature chair I got you from that weird diorama museum?"

"Of course I do! It's my good-luck charm. Not that I believe in luck or anything," I added.

"Well, bring it with you to that marine biology place. Maybe you'll see a mermaid."

"I don't believe in mermaids, either."

"Maybe you should," Gabriel said, grinning.

What Happened Next

What happened was that as soon as we got home, I talked to Mom and Dad, who e-mailed Ms. Molina, who called the landline early the very next morning, even though it was July 4.

"Zinny, I'm glad to hear you've reconsidered," she said kindly. "But I have to be honest with you—I'm a little worried. There were only a few slots in the program, and when you gave up yours, I'm sure they filled it right away."

"So you mean it's too late now?" I heard my voice shaking. Somehow between yesterday, when Gabriel had urged me to try, and this morning, I'd realized how much I needed to do this summer program. It felt necessary to me, like aeration in a tank.

"It may very well be too late," Ms. Molina admitted. "Although . . ."

"Yes?"

"What if you wrote an essay, or not an essay, maybe just a letter, explaining in your own words why you want to come? What you hope to get out of the summer—you know, all the reasons they should make an exception for you. Do it fast—this morning would be best, even though it's a holiday. And as soon as you've written it, e-mail it to me, and I'll forward it to the director."

"Okay." My heart was in my throat. "Do you think it'll work?"

"Honestly, Zinny, I can't promise. But think of it as a chance to share something about yourself with the world. Something important."

I went to my bedroom. Scarlett was sleeping over at Jamilla's house, so for once I had it all to myself.

I opened my laptop.

Share something about yourself with the world. Such as what? Really, there was too much to say.

So I figured I should focus on what Ms. Molina had

said—the important things. And pretend Mr. Patrick had covered the walls with white paper.

Dear Person Who Reads This,

My teacher Ms. Isabella Molina (Lakeland Middle School) told me to write to you explaining why I didn't accept the invitation to join the summer program at Blue Shoals, and also to ask if I could still get in. I know you had only a few spots and it was a privilege to get accepted, so I messed up when I said I wasn't going. The reason that happened was because my big brother was sick with a mental illness, and when he came home from his residential treatment center, I thought my family needed me to stay home this summer. It's not like I think he's all cured forever, and that there won't ever be anything to worry about again—but I can tell he's doing much better now. He says he really wants me to do Blue Shoals, and I believe him.

Ms. Molina says you are all full of students for the program, and probably don't have room for me anymore. I know the program is about to start very soon. But I think you should still let me in, because I love science, and this year I figured out something important about it. In Ms. Molina's class we observed and did experiments on crayfish. And what I learned was that even if you set up the best tank, with the best aeration, and feed your crayfish the best shrimp pellets, and give him rocks to climb on and plants (etc., etc.), he might still try to escape. You can't control everything, and you can't predict everything either.

The same thing with people.

I think this will make me a good scientist, knowing you should just keep your eyes open for everything. Because everything can happen.

Anyway, I hope it's not too late and you can still let me into the summer program.

Sincerely,

Zinnia Manning

And What Happened after That

The letter worked. A few days later I heard that I'd get to go to Blue Shoals after all. And like Ms. Molina predicted, it was the best summer of my life. But that's a whole different story from the one I'm telling you now.

I didn't see a mermaid, of course.

I saw real things.

Not trapped in fish tanks. Swimming in the big, beautiful Pacific Ocean:

Mantis shrimp and sea lions.

Turtles, seaweed, and octopi.

Anemones, stingrays, and starfish (one of them with six arms!).

And you know what I think?

No—you know what I *know*?

Everything in the world is part of nature. All the creatures, even the weird ones, are just figuring out how to grow, how to change. How to survive. And maybe they need some help, but if they do, that's okay. I think they'll be okay.

Because, like Aiden told me once, survival is realistic.

Acknowledgments

Once again, heartfelt thanks to my brilliant editor, Alyson Heller, for all the joyful collaborations over the years! Thanks to all the folks at Aladdin/S&S who make books possible: Mara Anastas, Valerie Garfield, Kristin Gilson, Michelle Leo, Chriscynethia Floyd, Chelsea Morgan, Sarah Woodruff, Amy Beaudoin, and Amanda Livingston. Karen Sherman, thank you for another terrific job of copyediting. Thanks to Jenna Stempel-Lobell for the beautiful cover art, and to Heather Palisi and Jess LaGreca for the design.

Ever grateful for my peerless agent, Jill Grinberg, and for the whole team at Jill Grinberg Literary Management: Katelyn Detweiler, Denise Page, Sam Farkas, Sophia Seidner, and Larissa Melo Pienkowski.

Thanks to Tracey Daniels, Casey Blackwell, and Karen Wadsworth of Media Masters Publicity for their inspired and tireless work.

Thanks to Dr. Jane Gaughran for chatting with me about bipolar disorder and its effect on siblings.

And to my real-life, actual, non-fictional family—Chris, Josh, Alex and Dani, Lizzy and Jamie—thank you for everything, always.

Here's a sneak peek at
B A R B A R A   D E E's
next novel!

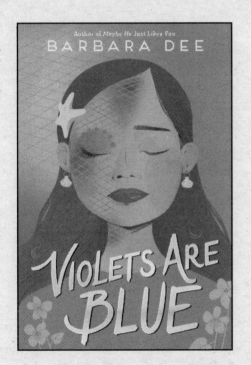

Author of *Maybe He Just Likes You*

B A R B A R A   D E E

VIOLETS ARE
BLUE

Click

Hey, guys, Cat FX here. Sorry if my voice sounds funny—my allergies are going full blast this morning.

Also, I couldn't sleep. So I spent the night thinking what I wanted to say to you, and here it is: It's really important not to overdo stuff, okay? Yes, I know it's exciting when you have all these shiny new products to play with, and you want to use everything all at once. But trust me on this, it's better to go slowly, adding layer on top of layer, building your character from the inside out. Know what I mean?

Also—and guys, I can't stress this enough— try not to be too obvious. Have fun with these techniques. Experiment, take risks, but always leave room for a bit of mystery.

Tonight my face was Seafoam Blue.

Not my whole face. Just a light swish across my forehead, the tops of my cheekbones, and around my chin.

The trick was to go slowly, like Cat FX said, applying layer on top of layer. Better to add than to subtract. Build the character from the inside out.

And to be who I imagined—my mental mermaid—I couldn't just slather on a ton of blue pigment. My mermaid's superpower was a kind of camouflage: blending into her surroundings. Slipping undetected through sunken ships. Escaping deadly sea monsters. Coming up for air when necessary.

The other thing I'd decided was that she was a collector. So when she won a battle, or discovered buried treasure, she would always decorate herself with souvenirs. To never forget what she'd been through, what she'd seen. To make it part of herself forever.

Which was why I was gluing a plastic pearl to my eyebrow when I heard the *GRRRRUUUNNNCCCHHH*.

My stomach clenched.

We'd been living here for almost three months, and I still couldn't get used to the awful grinding sound of the garage door.

But at least it gave me warning. Before Mom could get all the way upstairs, I tossed the jar of Seafoam Blue face pigment, the eye shadow in Cyber Purple, the waterproof eyebrow pencil in Medium Brown, and the spidery false eyelashes into my secret makeup kit. Then I slid it under my bed, all the way to the farthest corner, tossing in an old sneaker to hide it.

The shoebox marked *M* stayed on my desk. Visible.

I checked the clock. Only 8:35.

Mom clomped up the stairs in her thick-soled Jungle Mocs, which I'm pretty sure is the official footwear of ER nurses when they aren't wearing sneakers. Just in time, I beat her to the door of my bedroom.

"Hey, honeybee," she called as she reached the top step. In her wrinkled spearmint-green scrubs, she looked droopy, like a plant you forgot to water.

When she smiled, you could see how hard her face was working. "Is that the mermaid?" she asked, lightly touching my cheek.

"Yeah," I said. Mom could always tell the effect I was going for, even when I was in the middle of a character. "Although I'm not totally sure about the color."

"You're not? What's wrong with it?"

"I don't know. The Seafoam Blue seems wrong. Too greenish, maybe? And I'm not getting that shimmery underwater effect. I followed all the directions, but . . ." I shrugged. "It's not how I thought."

"Well, I think it looks really great so far. And I love that eyebrow pearl." She pushed her too-long bangs out of her eyes. "You finished your homework, Wren?"

"Yep. An hour ago."

She looked past me, into my room. Could she see the makeup kit under my bed? No, that was impossible. But of course she could see the shoebox marked *M*—on my desk, like usual.

"And did your friend Poppy come over after school?" Mom always called her "your friend Poppy," like she thought she needed to remind me that everything was different now: I had a real friend.

"Mom, Poppy has soccer. Remember I told you?" *At least twice. No, more than that.* "And why are you home so early?" *Again.*

"Another mix-up with scheduling. My supervisor keeps overstaffing." Mom leaned against my door and shut her eyes.

For a few seconds I just watched her. With all the changes in her schedule, I knew she hadn't been sleeping well. Not during the night, anyway.

So it didn't shock me to see her so tired. Still, it was a little awkward, both of us just standing there, not talking. Not moving.

"Mom," I said.

Her eyes fluttered open. When she took a step, her knee buckled, or something. She grabbed the doorknob to keep from falling.

"You okay?" I said quickly.

"I'm fine." A small wince. "Just my stupid knee acting up again. Don't worry about it, Wren. I have an early shift tomorrow, so I think I'll just take some Advil and get into bed. Will you please walk Lulu so she can pee?"

Lulu was our three-legged French bulldog. She peed sixteen times a day, and that's no exaggeration.

"Sure," I told her. "Go rest, Mom. And put a pillow under your knee."

"Hey, I'll be the nurse around here, not you." She threw me a little smile as she disappeared into her bedroom.

I waited, and then I heard it: *Click.*

One day while I was at school, Mom had a lock put on her door. To keep the cat off her bed, she'd explained. Although, really, that made no sense, because our one-eyed cat, Cyrus, was too old to jump that high anyway.

And now, every time I heard that sound—*click*—my heart flipped over, but I couldn't say why.

I returned to the mirror propped up on my desk, in front of the shoebox. The mermaid looked blurry now, out of focus, the Seafoam fading into boring pink skin.

And the funny thing about makeup effects? They were all just technique, Cat FX said, not magic. But sometimes if you stopped in the middle, it was like you were breaking a spell—and no matter how hard you tried, you couldn't get it back.

I wiped my face and went downstairs to get Lulu's leash.

Changes

There are two kinds of makeup effects: the kind that conceal and the kind that reveal.

As a makeup artist, I'm not about concealing. And I truly believe there's no such thing as a facial flaw or imperfection.

What I'm about—what I'm all about—is revealing something true. Something deep inside, that maybe you didn't even know existed. But that you need to share with the world.

The day Dad left us, just a little over nine months ago, it all happened fast. One gray Saturday morning in February, when we were still living in the house in Abingdon, I woke up to the sound of loud arguing in the kitchen. Yelling,

actually, which happened a lot those days, followed by a car zooming out of our driveway.

At breakfast Mom was drinking coffee in her favorite red mug and reading her phone. Just like she did every regular morning.

"Where's Dad?" I asked.

"Taking a Lyft to the airport," Mom said, still reading. "I'm sure he'll call you as soon as he can."

Were her hands shaking? Her face looked pale. Although she was looking down at her phone, so it was hard to be sure.

"What's going on?" My voice sounded like a five-year-old's, like a squeaky little mouse.

Mom looked up to give me a small, pinched smile. "We'll talk about it, Rennie. But later, because . . ." Her voice trailed off.

"You had a fight? With Dad?"

She didn't answer that specific question. Instead she stood and kissed my forehead. "I don't want you to worry, sweetheart, okay? Everything will be fine, I promise."

Then she put her mug in the sink and left the kitchen.

I waited at the table, but she didn't come back. In fact, I could hear her upstairs in her bedroom, opening and shutting dresser drawers, like she was searching for something, or maybe throwing things away. Pretty soon I figured out that she wanted to be alone, and that I shouldn't knock on her door to ask more questions.

I told myself that if something really serious or import- ant had happened, Mom would just come right out and tell me—wouldn't she? And wouldn't Dad, too? Besides, Dad traveled a lot for his job selling software to companies, so it wasn't completely strange that he'd taken a plane on a weekend morning. Although it *was* strange that he hadn't said goodbye; he'd never left without an early morning hug at the very least.

A few hours later my phone rang. And that was when my stomach knotted, because if my sort-of-friend Annika wanted to talk, she always texted. Mom did too, when she was at the hospital. So for a second I didn't even recognize my ringtone. That it belonged to me, I mean.

But it was Dad; he'd just landed at JFK, and was in a taxi on the way to Brooklyn.

"So Mom told you?" he asked.

"Not really," I said. "I think she's too upset. Dad, what's going on?"

He paused. "It's not something we should discuss over the phone."

Now my heart was banging. "Okay. So when exactly *will* we—"

"Rennie, Mom will talk to you and so will I, but in

person. And I'll see you very, very soon. We both can't wait for you to visit, jellybean. We'll show you around the city and have lots of fun."

He was using so many strange words that bounced off my brain like hailstones: "Visit." "Soon." "City." "Fun." But I picked just one.

"Who's 'we'?'" I asked.

"Me and Vanessa." The bad cell service made his voice sound whooshy, like he was going through a fun-house tunnel. Maybe he was. "The woman I met at that software convention in October. I think I mentioned we did a panel together . . . ?"

"No."

"Well, I'm sure I did, jellybean." Now I heard a sound like bubble wrap popping. And then: "We'll talk more later, in person. I love you very much. Always have and always will."

I was too shocked to answer. Had Dad ever told me about any Vanessa? I was pretty sure if he'd said something like, *Hey, jellybean, I've been hanging out with a woman WHO IS NOT MOM,* I'd have processed that information. Although maybe he'd said it in a way I didn't get. Or maybe I wasn't really listening.

"All right, gotta go now," Dad said. "I love you, Rennie."

"I love you too," I said. There was more crackling on the line, so I couldn't tell if he'd even heard it. But then my phone beeped, which meant the conversation was dropped anyway.

Mom was normalish for around a week. I say *ish* because how normal is it to not talk about a missing husband? But she didn't need to specifically tell me that she and Dad had broken up, because by now it was pretty obvious. One time I even said "when you get divorced"—just tossed the word "divorced" into the middle of a sentence, like a firecracker— and she didn't correct me, or even blink.

So I thought: *Okay, that's it, then. Divorce.*

After that first week she started marathon sleeping.

Being an ER nurse meant Mom had weird schedules that were constantly changing, so at first I didn't notice all the napping. But one day I left for school with her still in bed, and when I got home, she was fast asleep on the sofa, cuddled up with Cyrus, wearing pajamas from the night before. On our old kitchen phone were two messages from her supervisor: *Kelly, how's that flu? We need to know when you're coming back to work.* And: *Kelly, I tried your cell twice, but you aren't answering. I also left you three texts. Please return this call immediately—*

I poked Mom's shoulder. "What's going on?" I asked. My voice was loud enough to startle Cyrus, who jumped off the sofa to sit on my foot. "You have the flu?"

"No, just resting." Mom's voice sounded funny. Foggy or something.

"But you told your boss you had the flu? How come?"

Mom ignored that question. "Did your father call you?"

Sometime lately—I couldn't remember when—she'd stopped saying "Dad" and had started saying "your father."

I shook my head.

"Well, sweetheart, he wants you to visit. In Brooklyn. For spring break."

Spring break? That was only two weeks away!

My heart skittered. "He does? But how would I get there? Are you coming too?"

"No, of course not," she said softly. "Anyhow, you're almost twelve; you'll be just fine flying on your own. The flight attendants will watch out for you on the plane, and he'll be right there when you land."

"Okay." I swallowed. "But I won't go if you don't want me to."

Finally, Mom sat up. "Where'd you get that idea?"

"I don't know. Don't be mad, I'm just saying—"

"I'm not mad, Rennie. Anyway, you *have* to visit. He's your father."

She'd said it again: not "Dad," but "your father." A change that was small but felt very big.

About the Author

BARBARA DEE is the author of twelve middle-grade novels published by Simon & Schuster, including *My Life in the Fish Tank, Maybe He Just Likes You, Everything I Know About You, Halfway Normal*, and *Star-Crossed*. Her books have earned several starred reviews and have been named to many best-of lists, including the *Washington Post* Best Children's Books, the ALA Notable Children's Books, the ALA Rise: A Feminist Book Project List, the NCSS-CBC Notable Social Studies Trade Books for Young People, and the ALA Rainbow Book List Top Ten. Barbara lives with her family, including a naughty cat named Luna and a sweet rescue hound dog named Ripley, in Westchester County, New York.

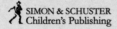

READ & LEARN

with *simon* kids

Keep your child reading, learning,
and having fun with Simon Kids!

A one-stop shop where you can
**find downloadable resources, watch interactive author
videos, browse books by reading level, and more!**

Visit us at
SimonandSchusterPublishing.com/ReadandLearn/

And follow us @SimonKids

75458

SIMON & SCHUSTER
Children's Publishing